THE CONSEQUENCES OF FALLING

LILIANA ROSE HASTINGS

Copyright © 2024 Liliana Hastings. All Rights Reserved.

No part of this book may be reproduced, distributed, or transmitted in any form, by any means, including photocopying or other electronic or mechanical methods, without the author's prior written permission, except in the case of brief quotations embodied in critical reviews.

This is a work of fiction. Names, characters, places, businesses, organizations, events, and incidents either are a production of the author's imagination or used fictitiously. Any resemblance to actual persons, living or dead, is unintentional and co-incidental.

Cover Design: Omniasstudiodesign | omniasstudiodesign.com
Editor: Emma Lounsbury | ejlediting.com
Formatting: Book and Moods

For those who yearn for the pure simplicity of love. For those who dream of gazing up at the stars, lost in a never-ending moment of longing. This is for those who crave love, above all else.

"When night fell, I listened to the songs that the moon and the stars were singing, and I sang with them. The world feels complete and whole, and I, its child, fit into it seamlessly."

— Susanna Clark, from Piranesi.

PLAYLIST

tape one; side a
i. sleep on the floor; lumineers/*ii.* coffee stained smile; delaney bailey/ *iii.* called you again; lizzy mcalpine/*v.* useless information; avery lynch/ *vi.* all i need; avery lynch/*vii.* simply the best; billianne/*viii.* home; catie turner/*ix.* matilda; harry styles/*x.* bigger than the whole sky; taylor swift/*xi.* in a week; hozier + karen cowley/*xiii.* touch; sleeping at last/*xiv.* milk and honey; billie marten/*xiv.* drops of jupiter; train/ *xv.* holocene; bon iver/*xvi.* hold back the river; james bay/*xvii.* blouse; clairo

tape one; side b
i. sweet; cigarettes after sex/*ii.* ivy; taylor swift/*iii.* sum of the in-between; maria kelly/*v.* firefly lullabies; ava beathred/*vi.* i know the end; phoebe bridgers/*vii.* saturn; sleeping at last/*viii.* anchor; novo amor/*ix.* sweet nothing; taylor swift/*x.* hate to be lame; lizzy mcalpine, finneas/*xi.* all of me wants all of you; sufjan stevens/*xiii.* right where you left me; taylor swift/*xiv.* northern attitude; noah kahan/*xvi.* i luv him; catie turner/*xvii.* astronomy; conan gray

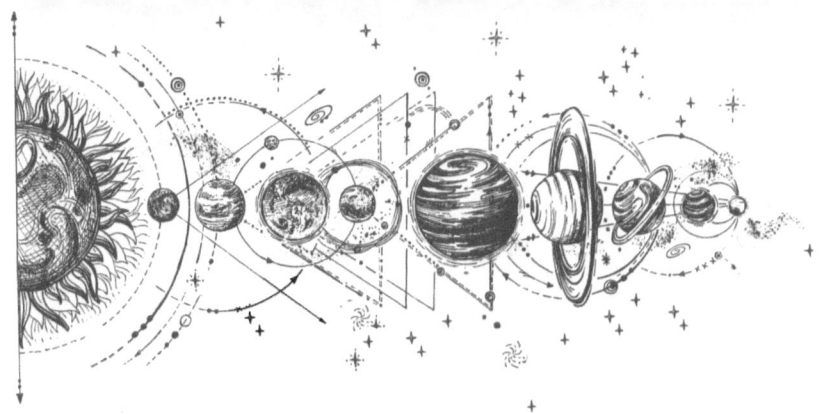

00.
cassiopeia

There is an art to falling in love. Akin to a gentle rain—soft, exuberant. Sort of like the ebb and flow of a wave. Delicate, rushed, haunting. When she was younger, she had never thought about how it would be to fall in love, never wondered how it would be to taste the lips of sweet redemption. Love was simply an afterthought—forgotten. There was an art to the vastness of love, the intricacy. Fleeting stares, staggered breathing, and dotted lines of constellations. Nova never gave much thought to love, not until him. Atlas Hale had been sudden, unannounced.

But he left Andromeda in his midst—stardust.

Atlas Hale was sudden, but she loves him all the same.

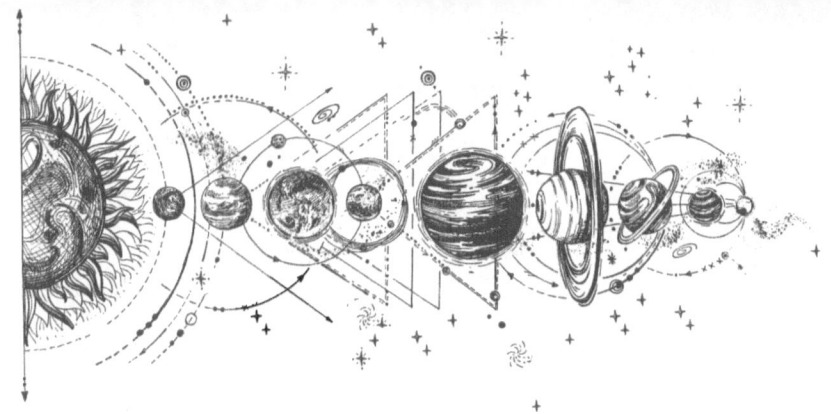

prologue
two years ago

Nova can't breathe.

She stands before the gathering, and finds herself gasping for air, a heaviness in her chest suffocating her. The priest's words, "From dust you came, and to dust you return," reverberate, but the voices around her become muddled, lost in the overwhelming chorus of grief. Tears stream down Nova's face, her cries echoing the pain within.

In the haze of sorrow, voices blend into an indistinct hum, the world around her fading as she grapples with the weight of loss. Indie wraps arms around her, whispering comforting words, but the ache persists. "It's okay," Indie reassures, yet in Nova's heart, the truth resounds – nothing is okay, and the fragments of a shattered reality may never

piece together again.

"It's okay," Indie whispers.

But it isn't.

It won't be, because she's gone.

Her mother is *gone*.

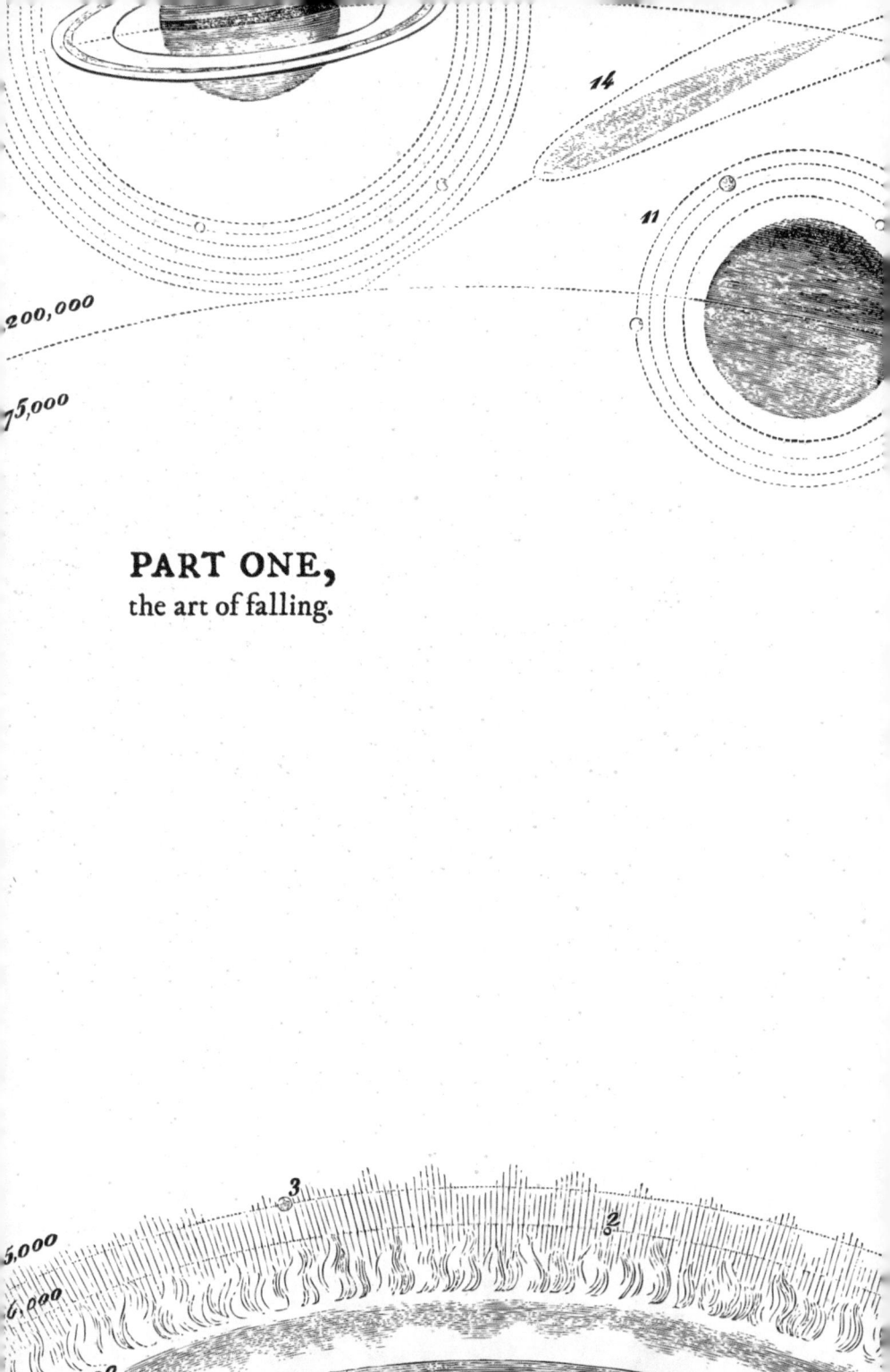

PART ONE,
the art of falling.

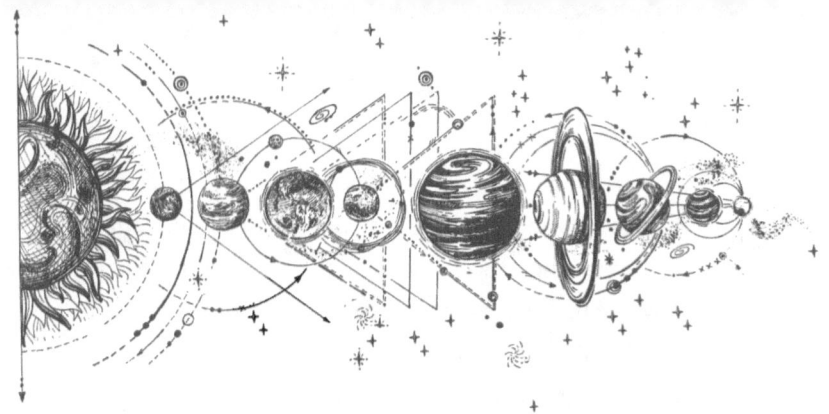

chapter one
under the overarching moon

The moon hangs low in the night sky, cocooned in white and amber hues, illuminating it. Below, trees sway, their embers flashing in the wind. Nova notes moments beneath the moon when she feels content—perhaps the reflection on cool park metal or the faint eeriness. Regardless, in these moments, Nova feels peace. A remnant of summer still whispers through the air, clinging to the earth's warmth, but autumn creeps in like a thief in the night—haunting, exuberant. The once warm sun's rays are replaced by looming clouds in the wake of fall. Nova embraces autumn, finding peace beneath its skies. She sighs, tilting her head back. From a young age, Nova was captivated by the stars; she finds camaraderie among them.

Her mother had once stated that there was stardust in the wind whenever Nova was near and that the brunette resembled a wayward fallen star. Nova assumes that was the reason behind her namesake. The stars had been added to family members in her mother's eyes. And

sometimes, Nova wonders if her mother is among the stars. Other times, she wishes to wield the thought like a sword and hurl it away. Thoughts of her mother seem to consume her mind recently—she misses her. Two years have passed since Nova's mother died; the good and bad memories associated with her seem to haunt Nova rather than bring her peace. When the thoughts become too much, she sits beneath the clouds at night, hoping that perhaps—if she wills it so—the stars will come down and capture her.

As Nova sits, a familiar pinch of aggravation tinges at her mind. Aggravation at her sadness, the sadness that never ends, and her pain that she cannot rid herself of. The rickety swing set echoes in her mind; it is a reminder of her mother, as are the vast majority of places within the desolate town. She comes to Chesterfield Park once during the year to reminisce, pay homage to her late mother, and escape from reality, if only for a moment. The old park sits diagonal to the bakeshop she had once visited daily. Now, though, not much. Most of the town has become a blur.

Tethered pain runs through each bricked building, and Nova struggles to exist among it. She cannot find room in the wreckage—it is consumed. The brunette runs a weary hand down her face, letting out a heaved breath. Sometimes, Nova wishes to be a star. As naive as the thought is, there are times, much like this, when Nova hopes that for a second, she could remove herself from reality and become a looming celestial being. The stars are constant, unchanging; the world, on the other hand, is neither.

Overhead, the moon looms—canting its head softly in the open wind, asking the questions that haunt her. The moon is a friend for the lonely and the brokenhearted. Beneath the light, under the overarching moon, there is a small, minuscule moment of reprieve. The fears and sadness that wrench her disappears for a moment.

And it is at that moment, that brief second of silence, that he appears. The soft incantation of his boots, the kaleidoscope of colors that etched within his eyes are a moment, a tethered thought, that Nova will never forget. His feet crunch above the smooth, dampened ground—each of his movements causing flurries of burgundy and orange to shudder beneath his feet. He clears his throat once and again before the obnoxious sound finally causes the brunette to turn her head. His eyes simmer beneath the overhead light—the first thing Nova ever noticed about him—and weariness lines his smile. Nova's hair falls to flurry around her, the wind causing the mahogany tendrils to escape her once patted and secured style. The man stands mere feet away; he wears his uncomfortableness on his face. Nova shifts in her seated position—her brow furrows as she takes him in further.

His hand is adorned with a cigarette, his head angling slightly as he pulls the end toward his mouth. The flick of his lighter sounds in the otherwise empty air. There is a faint crackle akin to a soft fire on winter's night; the sound dissipates, and the faint smell of smoke lingers. It carries in the air, cradling the once-fresh scent of pine and dew. Nova sniffs, her nose scrunching as the smell masks her senses. She contains her threatening cough. It is a free county after all—who is she to deny him suicide?

"Sorry." The soft baritone timbre within his voice causes her hands to tighten against her jean-clad thighs. "Am I bothering you?"

Yes, the word is tethering to her tongue, but instead she shakes her head once—twice. "No, I was about to leave, anyway."

"Don't—not on my account, at least," the man interjects.

"I would rather not die from secondhand smoke inhalation."

"Mm, but what a tasteful death it would be." The cigarette upturns with his lipped smile. He takes another drag, exhaling the smoke before dropping the stick lazily to the ground below. "Sorry," he offers.

"That's littering," she scowls, "but thank you regardless."

The man raises his brow, amusement washing over him. "You're welcome," he speaks tautly as he lowers himself.

An absence of sound engulfs them, creating an atmosphere of stillness. It isn't a calm or uncomfortable silence, but a state of existence. Nova is approached by a wave of fatigue as the night air wraps around her. She slowly sinks into the cool earth, taking a moment to bask in the tranquil radiance of the moon.

"I'm Nova," the brunette speaks quietly into the darkness.

"Atlas," he replies. *Did he know at that moment that his name would be tethered to her lips forever, much like a sacred prayer?*

"To suffer." Her lips press into a thin line as she winces. "Your name." She shifts. "It means to suffer. That's quite depressing, honestly."

He tosses her a careless smile. "I find it rather fitting."

She hastily pushes her glasses up, the accumulating sweat on her nose causing the dampening plastic to slip. His eyes, a soothing hue of blue, sparkle with curiosity as he returns her gaze.

"So," Nova's voice sounds in the silence. "I've never seen you here before."

"It's because I come on the days when you're not here."

"Oh." She snorts, her body turning slightly. "Is *that* the reason?"

Atlas hums, "Mhm."

She watches as Atlas raises from his seated position on the ground and lowers himself into the swing set that creaks and moans in protest from his weight. His movements still at the soft *pop* of metal; blue eyes meeting her own in an array of emotions—amusement, slight fear, and something else she cannot place. Nova stifles a laugh, shaking her head at his feigned worry. Despite the amusement that coats his face, his posture is slumped—almost defeated.

"You okay?" she finds herself asking.

"Peachy," he responds with a tight smile.

"Okay." She offers him a quaint smile in return.

"Okay."

Does he know that his 'okays' would soon become her salvation?

"Do you ever wonder how the stars are born?" Nova attempts to break the heaviness. Despite the irrelevancy and randomness of the question, the woman is slightly curious to hear his answer. "Do you think they appear out of nothing?"

Would they remember this as the moment everything shifted?

"The stars?" he repeats slowly.

"Yes. Do you not think about the stars?"

"No," Atlas speaks curtly. "Not really. They're just there."

"Nothing is just—there."

"Is there a point that you're trying to get to?" the man asks, his palm pressing against his sockets, willing the headache that was beginning to form behind his eyes to disappear.

"When I was small, my mother used to tell me that the sun and the moon kissed—and that was how the stars came about. She said there was this cosmic reaction to the eclipse, and the love shared between two forbidden lovers was enough to bind them together and that despite their longing, the moon always had a small piece of the sun."

Does she know that to Atlas, she will become a star?

There is a brief bout of silence. Thick and suffocating.

The moon leans overhead, whispering about her ears—telling the woman an endless story of how the stars sought out love and deemed it worthy; worthy that the rays of the moon shone fruitfully on it.

"Your mother is oddly poetic," Atlas speaks almost dryly. His voice is masked, void of emotion. "She's quite the dreamer."

Does he know that soon his dreams will be filled with her?

"Yeah." Her smile twists—waning downward. "She was."

He speaks no words because what can he say? Sorrys are lost and tired—-they offer nothing in return for the haunting sadness.

"It's her anniversary." Nova rises, far too consumed by her thoughts to care about the dampness on her rear. "That's why I'm here," she explains as she lowers herself into the swing beside him. "She used to bring me here a lot when I was a child, here I am."

"Here you are," he repeats softly.

Her brown eyes find his blue ones, a clash of colors—vibrant, dark, tethered, and worn. Taking advantage of the moment, the man's eyes flicker across Nova's face, taking in every detail. He can't help but notice the freckles that pepper her nose, adding a touch of whimsy to her otherwise serious expression. He also can't fail to see the flush of her cheeks, resulting from the chilly wind blowing through the area.

As his eyes continue to roam, he notices a tiny scar nestled just above Nova's eyebrow, a testament to some past injury or mishap. Despite its small size, it only adds to her charm, making her more approachable and down-to-earth. And then there are her lips, full and enticing, that curve upward into a radiant smile. Nova is beautiful, and the man can't help but be drawn to her like a moth to a flame.

"Look," her voice breaks his enchantment. "There is Sirius."

She points toward the luminescent beacon that called to the night. The bright star sits among the sea of specks but is far more promising than the rest. Hues of amber are exhausted around it.

"It's the brightest star you can see with the naked eye."

"I never noticed."

The silence settles within the marrow of her bones. Her entire life has been numbered in stars—she counts them, marvels at them. Infinities consume her whole life. She anchors to the moments spent beneath the stars, embracing the vast impasse above. There is solace, momentary, but solace nonetheless. In her mind, her mother is a star, and Nova counts them all in hopes that she will live among the infinite number of them. Her mother is infinity. Her mother is a star.

"Do you *think*—" His brow furrows. "Sometimes, I wonder if maybe there's more beyond the stars. Do you think that there's a world beyond this one? Somewhere where shit doesn't pile up every second."

"No," she murmurs. "Why would I want to live in a world without the stars—what does anything beyond them offer me?"

"Peace. The world is a fortress to the damned."

"Did you get that from a book?"

"No. Unfortunately, all of my afflictions are from my head."

"To *suffer* indeed," teases Nova.

Atlas sniffs, his gaze shifting to the ground beneath him. There is a stillness here—momentary, but stillness. It is quiet. The emotion is foreign, a lonesome friend, but beneath the moon, it is there.

"Without suffering, there'd be no compassion."

"Did you seriously quote *A Walk to Remember*?"

"Maybe." A smile teases his lips.

Nova shakes her head, a soft laugh escaping past her lips. Atlas notes that the sound resembles a wind chime—silky, delicate. The sound dances along the particles in the wind before finding solace in his ears. But he would not utter those words. He would hold them.

"Atlas." The name finds a home among the stars.

The man hums a response.

"Thank you for sitting here with me—even though you don't know me, your company has given me far less sadness."

He merely grunts in response.

"I should head home," Nova concurs.

Atlas nods. Once, twice.

"Tomorrow?" she questions. "Later, I guess?"

His feet dig into the ground below as he rises from his seated position. The shadow that falls over Nova causes her to retract slightly, and as she cranes her head to look up at him—she notes the soft freckles on his nose and the sharpness of his jaw. But despite the uncertainty that wrecks him, Atlas nods. His head tilts as his eyes roam her face, taking in the soft flush of skin that rose under his acquisition. He nods again, his hands treading through his pockets—clutching at the pack of cigarettes that burned against his thigh.

"Later."

The door rebounds against the frame as she enters the warm apartment. Her keys follow noisily in her wake. Nova lets out a haunting sigh as she places her purse on the hook near the entrance. Every moment that ticks by this day is shrouded in pain. Her footsteps echo softly against the wooden floor. The apartment is quiet, she assumes her roommates are still out. Flicking the light on, Nova stifles a yawn. Her fingers catch in her wild tendrils, balling at her scalp as she tugs softly, wishing to relieve some of the pressure accumulating at her temples. Nova trudges toward the refrigerator, yanking the door open. The dimmed light casts upon her face as she browses the selection until her eyes train on the small slice of cake in the far corner of the fridge. The sight of the cake causes her heart to shutter. *I miss you,* Nova thinks to herself. She closes the door with her hip, snagging a clean fork on her way toward the kitchen island.

The day had been long and restless. She only hopes that tomorrow would be far better—less looming. Her eyes tinge with tears at the thought. Nova swallows, attempting to halt the liquid that threatens to slide down her cheek. I *miss you, Mama*. She blows out a breath as she lowers to the barstool. The large slice of lemon cake stares back at her. It had been her mother's favorite. The buttercream frosting has hardened from the time spent in the refrigerator, but she hardly cares. It reminds Nova of her.

Happy anniversary, Mama, she thinks.
I love you

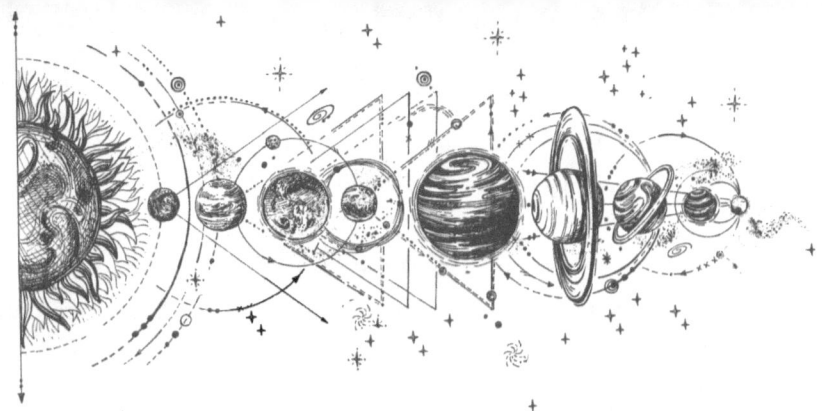

chapter two
andromeda

Two months pass, and Atlas still remembers the soft perfume that lingered in her wake. He is not sure what to make of her—Nova. She came in as quickly as a stumbling child and disappeared suddenly with promises of another interaction left hanging in the air.

Perhaps that was why he could not find it within him to return.

He has never been fond of tomorrows. The sentiment is far too deep, too promising. Atlas Hale resembles a fallen leaf, caught in the wind and constantly drifting. He is a fleeting entity. That is who he will always be. His feet crunch atop the dried leaves that coated the ground, each step leading him back to the small park on the edge of town. As he returns, there is a stillness, a pungent familiarity, almost a sense of déjà vu. The town is historical, dripped in history—woven around every corner, but the park is an anomaly among the other dusted and bricked buildings. Sailor Ridge is home, sort of. Atlas has not been

able to identify what was to be considered home for as long as he could remember.

Sailor Ridge is a town that creeps under the shadows of others. Washington State is dreary during the autumn season. Sometimes, at night, it resembles a horror movie. Other times, the orange-yellow glow of the overhead street lights makes the town seem almost magical. His mouth screws up, fighting a frown as he shuffles toward the rickety swing set; his backpack swinging noisily behind him, disrupting his otherwise quiet journey. The time is nearing Halloween. Somehow, the year has ticked by, and he has not noticed a thing.

Atlas can't remember much about the passing months, no memory quite memorable enough to stick out among the others. Although Nova appears to be a thought he cannot shake away. He could not attempt to return in the months that passed, not that he much wanted to. There was something sticky, almost unnerving, about the quiet that filled his mind in her presence and the tranquility that appeared in the park Atlas now stands in. As he lowers himself onto the ground, he remembers her here—leaned back beneath the waning moon, basking in the light.

Nova seems to be unpredictable, odd, and Atlas—he hates it.

Rummaging through his bag, the man seeks out the fresh pack of cigarettes that he shoved inside during his haste to leave the small convenience store. Murray's is a normalized staple in Sailor Ridge. His palm rests against the butt of the package, tapping it once—twice, before the loud ripping of the plastic film fills the night air. Atlas knows they are terrible—they kill, but most pleasurable things are demons to the soul, right? That was what his father said before ruining his kidneys with alcohol. Perhaps he is indeed his father's son, after all. An unamused snort escapes him at the thought. *Yeah, right.*

He shakes his head as he raises the slim stick to his mouth, his free hand reaching to rummage for his pocket lighter.

"Is this how we're always going to meet?"

His exhale is loud, exaggerated, at the sound of her voice. The man lets the cigarette hang loosely in his mouth as he squints at her. Her brow is raised, and her gaze filled with judgment. Atlas nearly rolls his eyes at her comment, but instead, the man releases a shuddering sigh. Removing the cigarette from his mouth, the blue-eyed man sends her a tight-lipped smile, nodding in acknowledgment.

"Nova," he responds.

"Those do kill you, eventually," Nova comments.

"Not soon enough," he mutters, slipping the stick back into the small pack. "What are you doing here?" the man questions.

He takes in her attire—the burnt orange sweater complements her skin tone, bouncing off the nearby light. She wears, in contrast, a pair of blue jeans, a darker blue than her paired Converse, covered with drawn stars. But what stands out the most is the unruly amount of dog hair that sticks to every inch of her. As he tilts his head, Nova seems to understand his question.

"I work at a dog shelter," Nova explains. "Hence the dog hair."

"Ah." He nods.

There is a moment, a brief lapse in the air that is fueled by tethered silence. Atlas leans back against his hands, frowning. There are moments steeped in silence wherever Nova was near; it is as though his mouth refuses to gain air and expel sound.

"Are you going to ask a question?" Atlas cuts through the silence.

"No, I was wondering what you were doing."

He asks her unamused, "What does it look like?"

"Sarcasm is rude," she points out.

"So, is asking strangers too many questions."

She pauses once more before speaking. "You never came back."

"Yeah, I was told not to talk to strangers growing up. Sorry."

"But you're here now—what's the difference?"

"I don't know," the man shrugs. "There's nowhere else to go."

"Can I sit?" She motions to the ground.

"No," he says curtly.

She rolls her eyes, sliding her bag onto the ground before following suit. "That was not convincing, you know?"

The clambering of her bag causes the man to wince. The closeness of her body in proximity to his own makes him itch. He shifts uncomfortably, leaning away from the heat that radiates from her. Atlas inhales deeply, his jaw tightening as she hummed beside him.

"Stop," he grinds out. "The humming—stop it."

"It's been stuck in my head all day, sorry," she says sheepishly.

"Stop. I came here for silence, not for a concert."

Her apology is soft, gentle—saddened.

He rubs a tired hand down his face, returning his attention to the sky.

"Can I ask what you are looking for?"

A meteor to come out and kill me, he thinks.

"—tell me about them," he interrupts. "The stars. Tell me about them again."

Atlas has been tired, and there has been a hovering weight over his chest that he can't seem to remove, except for that one night. There was peace there. Momentary, but it was peaceful.

Her head cants as she peers over her shoulder to glance at his slain position. His hands are crossed over his stomach, and his eyes are glued to the impasse of blue that coated the night sky. In her movements, Nova's hair fans around her, resembling a mousy blanket. She chews softly on her bottom lip before turning to face the nearby slide.

"Andromeda," she starts. "It's the closest galaxy to the Milky Way, the unique and beautiful thing I have ever seen."

Atlas says nothing, his silence urging her on.

"It is the most distant object that can be seen with the naked eye, like Sirius, the one from last time," she continues. "Oh, and then there's Canopus. It's older than the sun, which is insane to think about. It was my mom's favorite star—but I think Capella is better. It means she-goat, and when I was younger, for some reason, it was the funniest thing in the world to me." Nova laughs, shaking her head.

Somehow, Atlas, too, finds himself laughing.

"I told my entire first-grade class that there was a star named after a goat, and I was serious about it—no one could shut me up."

Soon, the laughter dies out, giggles dissolving into the night, becoming whispers in the wind. Atlas hates it. Because camaraderie with strangers is a walking disaster, because the stars have no place in his thoughts—he doesn't deserve them. Because to laugh freely feels like his chest is constricting and will explode in moments. He pushes himself into a seated position, his chest starts to heave. He stares into the distance, letting his hand fall limply onto the grass. He hates the stuffiness, the silence that evens out. He hates how easily the conversation began and how naturally it has ended. Because strangers are strangers, and one meeting is simply one meeting.

Atlas Hale is not one for friends or acquaintances. He finds no need for many of them—his friend is Murray, the convenience store owner. His friend is the cat he fed on his way to work daily—and Damien, whom he has known for his entire lonely life. That is enough. He needs no more.

"I should go," Atlas says into the night. "It's getting late."

Nova glances up in confusion as he stands abruptly.

"Oh, okay." She nods, reaching for her bag.

He slings his backpack over his shoulder, his left hand clutching the singular cigarette from earlier. Bringing the stick to his lips, he starts rummaging through his pocket to retrieve his lighter.

"Um, this was nice. We should hang out again."

The faint crackle catches in the air; he inhales the smoke burning his throat before exhaling, a cloud of gray surrounding the pair.

"Unlikely. But thanks for the chat."

"Did I overstep?" she asks.

"No," is his only response. "See you around, Nova."

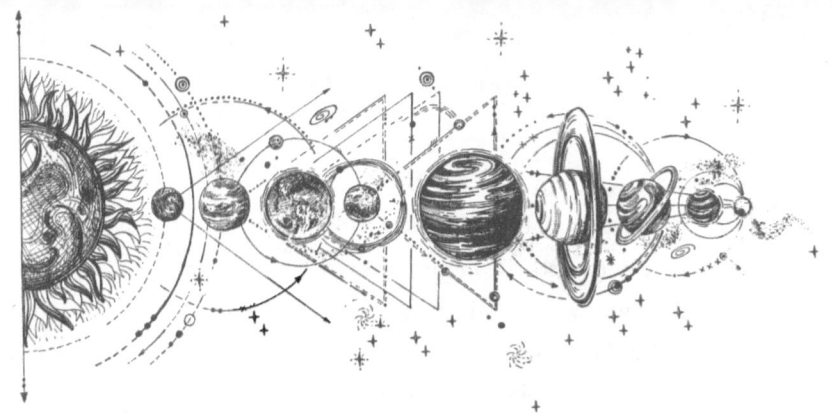

chapter three
murrays convenience store.

Murray's sits cocooned among the sea of desolate buildings—each brick ticked with drips of rain and washed leaves. In a storm that refuses to cease or give him a reprieve, Atlas finds solace in a local convenience store. Classic. Perhaps it is a tad bit sad, ultimately. The outside air brushes the back of his neck, the shifting temperatures causing the hair to rise against his flushed skin. The faint smell of greasy hot dogs swirls about his nostrils, and the familiar drawl of saliva that accompanies it returns with passion. The store is quiet, as usual, though the warmth that engulfs him is new.

He attributes it to the looming cold that carries outside. Rows upon rows of candies and processed snacks line the perimeter of the store—the empty cart corral near the front holds crates instead. Murray's is old, as ancient as the town it sits in, but Gerald Murray keeps the small store to the best of his ability. The familiar scent of peppermint and

cigarettes exhumes from near the front register.

His hand snags a battered basket in his saunter, the plastic holder swinging back and forth in communion with his steps. Atlas knows the store like the back of his hand; he has spent much more time there than he wished growing up. The memories of his drunken father perched against the bricked wall outside are forever burned into his retinas and etched through every inch of the building. He exudes a scoff at the thought, shaking his head. Sniffing, Atlas throws a candy bar into the basket—along with two packs of gum. His eyes wander the surrounding area, scouting for the soft drink that always quenches his thirst. The vanilla-flavored soda leaves a bitter aftertaste in his mouth, but Atlas still indulges in the liquid despite it.

"All out." Murray's grovel is familiar, aged.

"Course you are." Atlas glances over at the older man. Shaking his hand, he snags a water instead. "Good day today?"

Because Murray, despite his kind smile, is riddled with grief.

"The sun is still shinin', ain't it?" he counters.

Because despite his pain, Murray always sees the sun.

"Here." Atlas retrieves the paper from his pocket. "It's not much. But there's enough. I can get back to you next week, too."

"You ain't have to do this."

He does. Because his father's bile still stains the laminated flooring despite the days and days of scrubbing. Murray walked him home every night since he was ten and made sure to lock the door behind him, bringing him a single candy bar for every birthday.

Atlas says nothing because the sentiment is well read.

"Those make you sick," Murray comments, shifting the conversation. "Them sticks ain't doing nothing more than killin' you."

"All great pleasures come with a price, Murray. Come on, old man, you know this." Atlas scolds as he places the pack into the basket.

"The price is death, you ninny."

Snorting, Atlas pushes back against the freezer door. "Mhm."

Waving him off, Murray pockets the money. "I'll be in the back. Holler if you need me. You know where the bags are, kiddo."

And then he is left alone again, with his thoughts—with the faint scent of lilies and lilacs that cling to his clothing from being in her presence. Her laughter still hangs in the air, and the disappointment that causes her features to age swirls around within his head. Nova is an entity unlike anything that he has ever seen before.

Frowning, his once sunny disposition is haunted by his inner turmoil. Atlas sits the basket on the counter, shuffling his things out. The crinkle of the cheap bags fills the air. The man shouts over his shoulder as he moves toward the door—goodbye written in the air. The automatic doors squeak open in his abandon, and soon, he is met with the crisp autumn air. The streets are empty, though the occasional car can be heard in the distance. From his previous location, Murray's was a short walk—not far, but the rain still managed to leave his shoes dampened despite it. In the distance, the park can be seen in the brush. From his squinted glance, Atlas can see her—Nova. She sits in the exact place as before—this time, her silhouette is hunched, almost as though she is contemplating something.

His legs move toward the park—his car is parked near the curb. Atlas wonders if she will see him. He wonders if perhaps she will smile as she had before. But as their eyes lock as he nears his car, she only looks at him with confusion. But what can he offer her? Because he, too, understands nothing of his previous actions or attitude toward her. Instead, he finds himself lifting his hand, the wave tumbling out of him.

She, in response, tilts her head—which confuses him.

But it isn't until the gentle call of her name reaches his ears that

Atlas realizes her gaze was not meant for him at all.

Perhaps she is not the one in need of a friend after all.

Perhaps Atlas is the one without companionship?

Perhaps his only companion is the convenience store's bricked building and laminated flooring.

chapter four
orion, margot's cafe, and tomorrows

There are moments, Nova noted, when the moon resembles a thumb. Perhaps the sentiment is odd, but the young woman can see it. When she tilts her head slightly to the left and squints—the moon appears almost dented in shape, as though it is a thumbprint cookie. In her mind, the moon's craters are filled with strawberry jam and coated in flurries of powdered sugar to taste. Despite the oddness, Nova thinks the moon is radiant that night.

Among her admiration, the soft echo of rain accompanies the murmurs and whispers filling the quaint coffee shop she frequents. Margot's Café sits among the sea of otherwise empty and rented buildings. The small space pairs as a coffee shop and a makeshift bookstore—selling secondhand books and an array of baked goods.

The faint smell of fresh baked goods bounces and molds to the air around her; it is comforting. Sometimes, if she sits long enough, the scent lingers within her clothing, perfuming the fabric. Perched against

the booth, Nova sits hunched in her position, the rough texture of her jeans snagging against the grooves within the table. Among the sea of exhausted yawns, Nova feels much like an anomaly—she sticks out. She appears almost naive in comparison in a room filled with hung suit coats and purses far more intricate than her tattered tote and paint-splattered jeans. Where their shoes are dusted in black, darkened in need to fit in inside courtrooms or offices, her own are stained, covered in wayward scribbles and stars. Growing up, Nova was always told to cling to her youth; her grandmother had once spoken about how sacred it was—important. Now, Nova wonders if perhaps childishness is an eventual curse rather than a faithful gift. Is she damned by childhood?

The world is a fortress to the damned—Atlas's previous words stumble within her mind. Perhaps Atlas was correct. The world is unkind to most of its inhabitants. There is no mercy here.

Sighing, Nova returns to her randomized scribbles. She has come to Margot's around the same time these past few years, retracing the steps of her mother and visiting the places that she had once held dear. Nova can remember spending countless nights here with her mom—face covered in the residue of blueberry pie and fingers stained with markers from her kid's menu coloring. Those were simpler times before the world showed its ugly head. Reality can be daunting, pitiless.

"Hey," his voice interrupts her thoughts. "Can I sit?"

Nova glances up at him, confusion lingering on her face. As her eyes roam she notes the dampness of his shirt and how it clings to his body; the soft scent of musk that mixes in with the fresh smell of rain engulfed her senses. She swallows thickly, nodding as she gestures to the seat opposite herself. *Yes*, it lingers on her tongue, but she cannot expel the word from her mouth. Instead, she figures her nod would do fine enough.

The thin coating of plastic covering the booth squeaks in protest as he lowers himself down and slides toward the window. In the quaint booth, he appears rather large; his muscles bulking as he shifts, attempting to grasp comfort in his hunched position. He clears his throat uncomfortably, trying to gather her attention that appears to be locked to his chest. Atlas tilts his head, his blue eyes shifting beneath the orange-yellow light above. His eyes slowly travel down the exposed column of her neck before returning to her face.

Nova has never seen him this closely, not within decent lighting. As she takes in his face, beneath a scrutinizing gaze, Nova feels the familiar rush of blood coat her cheeks. He is attractive. Very attractive. His dampened dark locks cling to his forehead, curling at the ends, and his face—Nova notes that he has a hot face. Chiseled and far more manly than she had expected. His face with the faint remnants of stubble, his lips—pink and plump—sits down and turns into a frown.

"Havin' fun?" he asks dryly, his index finger tapping impatiently against the table. "Are you done?" he questions once more.

She blinks. Once, twice. "What?" she speaks breathlessly.

"Are. You. Done?" he repeats, emphasizing each word.

"No, uh, sorry." She clears her throat. "Sorry."

"You said that already," Atlas notes as he leaned back.

Nova wanted to die. "Right. Uh, how are you?" she opts.

Amusement wanes on his face, his eyes brightening as he takes in the flustered woman. He notes that her hair is pulled back into a low ponytail, and she wears a sweater—it was men's. His brow raises as he crosses his arms over his chest, straightening, and his amusement flees.

"So, where's your boyfriend?" he finds himself asking.

She furrows her brow. "I'm sorry?"

"The guy from the park yesterday."

She blinks, confused. "You mean Rowan?" She speaks slowly. "When did you even—are you stalking me, or something?"

"Mm." Atlas shakes his head. "No, that would imply interest."

"You seem interested enough," she shoots back.

"Stalking implies care and obsession. I have neither of those as it pertains to you, Nova. Do not flatter yourself," the man dismisses her.

"You are truly a ray of sunshine," she replies dryly.

He scoffs in reply.

There is a silence here—thick, almost suffocating. Between the pair, no words are spoken for quite some time after. Atlas leans toward the window, appearing deep in thought as his finger trails after fallen raindrops on the cool glass. Nova, instead, watches him with curious eyes—questioning, attempting to grasp his exact need for being here.

"I can feel my skin burning, you know," he grumbles.

"I'm sorry, that was rude." Nova ducks her head.

As he runs his finger along the edge of the table, Atlas watches her, noting the discomfort that seems to line her eyes. He tilts his head again, taking in the way she pulls nervously at her sleeves—tugging, more like yanking on the wool material. In the midst, his hand itches to remove her own.

"Stop," he notes her confusion. "It's a nice sweater. You wouldn't want to ruin the material from tugging like that."

"I'm cold, that's all," Nova defends.

Atlas hums a response, his eyes still training on her hands.

"What are you doing here, Atlas?"

The question hangs tautly in the air.

Because he has not a single clue.

Because his feet seemed to accelerate when he spotted her from across the street—like some creepy wannabe stalker.

"I don't know," the man admits.

There is a brief pause.

"You confuse me," he blurts out. "I don't understand how you see the world the way that you do. Like it's not horrible. Like people aren't dying or that there aren't wars breaking out. You talk about it as if there's actual goodness in it. I don't get it."

Her eyes soften at his confession. "The world is beautiful." She speaks with so much conviction that momentarily, briefly, Atlas finds himself almost believing her. "Though I can't say the same for the people in it, there is nothing wrong with the earth. It feels rude to blame it for the mistakes of the people that inhabit it."

"That is hauntingly naive," Atlas points out, shaking his head.

She frowns. "I'm not naive. I am aware of how sick the world is, how unkind—frankly, I have no choice but to, having experienced it myself. Finding the beauty within something is not naive."

Beneath the light, as their hands seem to inch closer, the man becomes increasingly more aware of their differing skin tones, how pale his looks compared to the olive hue within her own. The soft layer of light brown contrasting the hints of pinks that linger on his skin—blue veins, seem muted among her green. He looks up at her, his mouth forming a tight line—because what else can he say?

"Anyway," she continues, waving him off. "There is some peace in life. I find my own in the stars, in books, or movies. I think that once you find something that brings you peace, the world will become much more bearable."

"Maybe."

"Oh, come on." Nova flicks his hand. "You have to enjoy something—anything. What's your favorite book?"

Atlas stares at his hand as though it were an inanimate object rather than flesh and bones. "I like quiet, when people don't speak," he grumbles, retracting his hand. "We should try that out—right now."

"You're pretty talkative to me."

He deadpans. "You seem to bring out the worst in me."

"My apologies," she smirks. "How rude of me."

Teasing is unusual to him. Atlas doesn't have many friends or acquaintances to tease or joke around with, so the sentiment is odd compared to his usual, more serious conversations. He talks among his coworkers. But those are far more logistical and intellectual conversations. This is different.

Noting his discomfort, Nova opts to change the subject.

"Did you know that the constellation Orion is named after a hunter from Greek Mythology?" She offers the fact randomly.

At her words, the tension in his brow seems to ease slightly. His silence beckons her forward. He leans his head against the cool glass, watching Nova speak animatedly, her hand waving around as she babbles about the constellation. She talks about how it was located within the celestial equator and visible from anywhere in the world. Atlas listens. The soft mewl of her voice is soothing.

"And funny enough, in the mythology, the seven daughters of Atlas are chased by Orion after becoming the object of his affection."

That particular fact makes him chuckle softly. "Of course."

Despite herself, Nova finds herself commenting on his laugh, how nice it sounds—deep. It is restrained within his chest, caught.

Perhaps that is the moment that he shuts down, or maybe it is when Atlas finds himself becoming wishful for another smile. Or when the tightness in his chest seems to loosen the longer he dwells in her presence. At some point in their exchange, his features became clouded, Nova noticed. Regardless of the quaintness, his smile has disappeared, and the lingering thickness in the air returned.

"Atlas?" She speaks his name among his crowded thoughts.

"Hmm?" He blinks.

"You okay?"

"M'tired. It's been a long day."

Silence.

"You're going to leave, right?"

"It's late," is his response.

"Half-past nine is not exactly late."

"Then it's raining." His mouth upturns to a slight smile.

"You might run out of excuses, eventually."

"Nah." He plays with a discarded napkin. "Doubt it."

"We're friends right?" she asks quietly. "I mean, sort of."

His movements still—and his gaze breaking from the table to land on her face. Her eyes are hopeful and determined, whereas his own are sunken and jaded. Her smile is soft and considerate compared to his face, which is set in stone, rigid. Atlas swallows thickly. His nod is stiff—uncertainty slithered through his vertebrae. Because to Atlas, friendship has never been an option he ever wants. He is content in his loneliness, always has been, but perhaps friendship wouldn't hurt?

Nova notes that he looks almost skittish—akin to a scared boy.

There is a momentary silence before either speaks again, and for a second, she regrets even proposing friendship. It may be too odd.

The pair are in an awkward staring competition, itching and waiting for one or the other to speak. Atlas lets his eyes drift, taking in the creases in her brows, the promise and hope that tethered to every blink. There is an innocence in Nova that he has not encountered since the womb—perhaps even before then. Not since before he was a speck.

"We're a bit too old for that, no?" He shifts uncomfortably at his own words. "I don't really hang out with people—not much outside of work."

"That's okay."

"And I don't text much. We have mouths for a reason."

"Valid argument."

"We are acquaintances."

"Sounds fair enough." She shrugs.

"I don't need to be fixed, or whatever it is you think this is."

His following words somehow promote her gentle touch, which causes him to flinch away—casting his eyes downward. His nostrils flare at the sudden rise of her scent due to her movements.

"Am I free to leave, or would you rather prevent me from sleeping further? Normal people deserve at *least* nine hours."

"Seven, *actually*." His glare burns her skin. "That was your attempt at a joke, right? We will be working on that."

Rubbing a tired hand down his face, the man hurries toward the end of the booth, "Goodbye, Nova." The words mix with a groan.

"Tomorrow," she corrects. "If we are going to be friends, I insist you say tomorrow instead of goodbye. Those are too final."

She figures it's because the last words her mother had ever spoken to her were *'goodbye.'*

Because her mother had truly meant it.

Because goodbyes are set in stone.

Sighing, Atlas says. "Tomorrow."

As he turns to leave, the man shutters in his movements, "Let me walk you out." It is not a question, much rather a demand of sorts.

"Oh no, that's fine—I was going to sit for a bit."

Atlas shoots her an annoyed look. "I don't like talking, which means my offer must be serious if I'm wasting my breath."

She rises from her seated position slowly. "Thank you."

He nods in response, gesturing toward the door. He is gentlemanly enough to allow her to walk before him—*his mother*, Atlas, inhales sharply at the thought. Frowning, he reaches over the shorter woman's head to open the door. Her soft praise of gratitude fills his ears. As they continue to walk, their shoulders brush, and though brief, Nova appreciates the warmth radiating through her body at the contact. The sidewalk is dampened from the rain, and large puddles accumulate on the ground below—Nova finds the town to be most beautiful when it rains. She thinks that it resembles a movie on nights like this.

"Where is your car?" Atlas asks as they rounded the corner.

"Oh, uh, it's over there." Nova points to the small Honda parked against the curb. Leaves covered it, but the light gray, almost metallic-looking Sedan is noticeable from a distance. "I can walk the rest."

He nods, once—twice. The man rocks awkwardly on his heel, his hands shoved into his dampening coat pocket as he waits for her to speak again. He can't find the words.

"I'll see you around?" Hopefulness douses her words.

"Mm." He gives her a rather curt nod.

"Tomorrow?"

The moon hangs overhead, and the rain starts to weaken with every second the pair stands. Even in the awful lighting, she makes autumn look far more beautiful. He notes how her eyes disappear as her smile rises, the freckles that pepper and kiss her skin—Atlas sees swirls of coffee inked with creamer in her eyes. A hope, a promise. Friendship.

"Tomorrow."

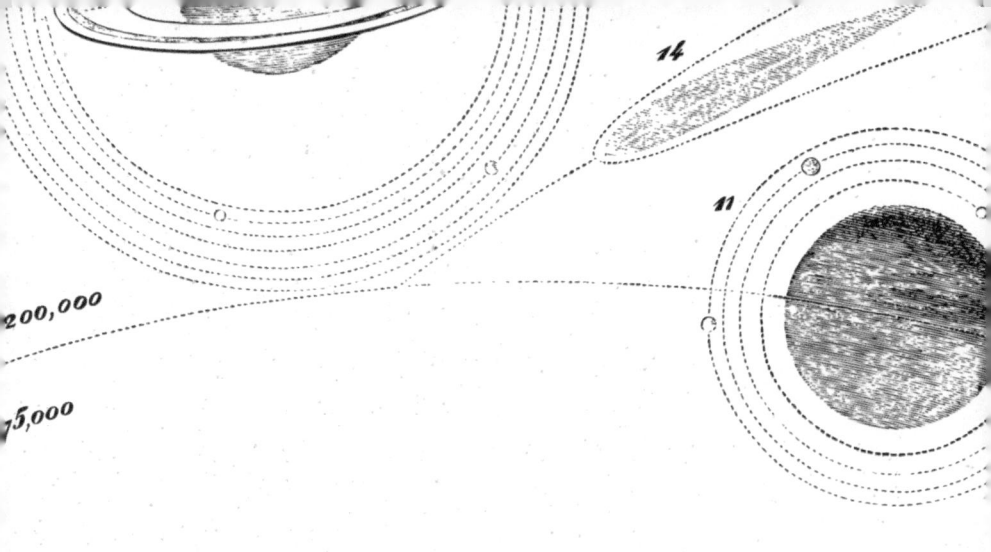

INTERLUDE
fleeting beginnings

he has not returned.
three weeks have gone,
and she has yet to run into him again.
beginnings are fleeting, and so is he.

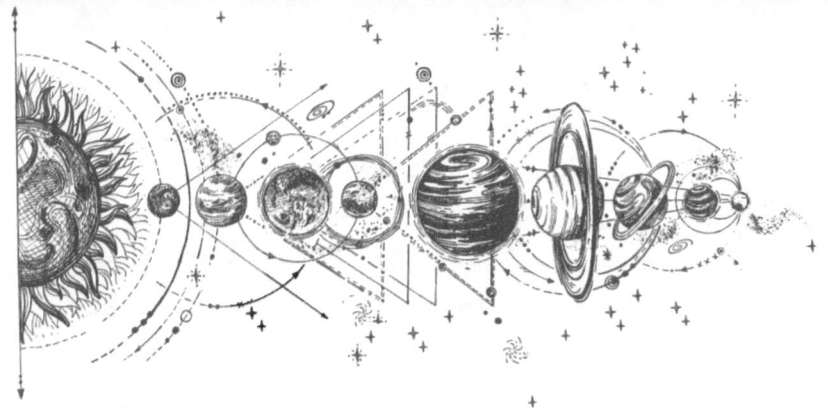

chapter five.
goodnights, indie, and dorothea's inn.

Sailor Ridge is whimsical among the cool autumn breeze and the heavy bout of fog. It is moments like these when the sun peeks out briefly to kiss and warm the sky if only for a second, Nova misses her mother the most. She misses her scent, a mixture of florals and aurora. Nova misses the gingham patterned skirts she wore no matter the occasion. Her smile was once faint—hidden, but when Marjorie smiled, it was breathtaking and luminescent. But among the smiles and laughter, there was a slither of pain that tainted her irises. A deepening sigh of *help* written along her lashes with every flutter. Her mother had hidden behind smiles, hope, and laughter. She hid her pain within *I love you* and forehead kisses.

Then, as quickly as she smiled, she fled.

Two years have passed, yet Nova swears she can still hear her laugh whenever the wind blows. Her mother is perpetually tied to autumn.

Perhaps that is why she loves it so much. Sighing, she tucks a loose thread of hair behind her ear. The air within the room has grown far colder—the revolving movements of tourists frequenting the inn fueling it further. Dorothea's Inn is a quaint building, housing merely forty rooms. The inn is a staple for the town; it's a money magnet, occupied primarily by tourists around the fall and winter seasons. Sometimes, before her parents divorced, the trio had taken stay-cations here at the inn—it was fun when she was younger, but now not so much. The rooms are far stuffier, filled with memories that plague her thoughts. But she comes every year, staying in the same corner room closest to the town square. Nova sits, the quilt that layers the bed scratching at her skin—but she sits, and she remembers.

The quiet is suffocating, more so than the memories themselves. It's odd how much of her mother runs through this town. How much of her still lingers within every single building. She is everywhere. A deepened frown appears on her face at the thought. Grief is a friend, a haunting, laughing, and taunting friend. But she had become far too acquainted with it the further she goes in life and the more everyone that she loves and cares for seems to leave her.

"Nova." Indie's voice drowns out the wreckage.

Indie, more often than not, takes the small trip with her to the inn. Around the same time every year, the pair takes off work and spends the entire week there. Indie isn't pushy; she doesn't question much. The vibrant woman knew her mother about as well as she had. The pair were friends for as long as they can remember, meeting once on the first day of kindergarten, and the rest is history. Indie understands. She doesn't press. She doesn't pry. Indie understands, and that is enough.

"Hmm?" she replies, breaking her gaze from the quilt before her.

Indie sends her a tight smile. Her eyes share the same worn and weathered look as Nova's. "Let's take a walk. I'm getting hungry."

"You can go, I'm fine." She dismisses her.

"Nova." A fallen curl flutters as Indie tilts her head. "You have to eat. Besides, Sienna made sandwiches for lunch again."

Where there is Indie and Nova—there is Sienna O'Connell, much like a braid, weaved and woven. The three are inseparable. They came to know Sienna years after meeting each other. In the second year of high school, Sienna O'Connell decided to brace the small town of Sailor Ridge, Washington, with her eccentric presence. Blonde hair resembling the ripest wheat and a smile that seems to shine brighter than any other—Sienna is the kindest soul: a party fanatic, but kind.

Sienna works in the conjoining building next to the inn. It is a local shop owned by her family. *Connie's* became a staple the second they arrived in town a few years ago. Sienna and her family are originally from New York, so the restaurant is about as close to the East Coast as Nova has ever had the chance to get. They sell deli-style sandwiches—the ones with the tiny toothpicks pricking the bread. Accompanied by a side pickle and some of the best in-house potato chips Nova has ever tasted.

Nova runs a tired hand down her face, sighing. "Okay."

She sniffs as she slid off the bed, shrugging on her jacket. As much as she wishes that her horrid mood is a result of this place alone, this town tied to her mother, Nova knows it has everything to do with him.

Atlas seems to come and go like a rushing wave. He is the least secure person that she has ever encountered. There is nothing remotely constant about him. But yet, she still craves his friendship.

Indie closes the door softly behind them. "So," the shorter brunette begins. "Do you want to tell me what else is going on?"

Because Indie knows her, she knows her better than anyone.

"No"—a forced laugh catches in her throat—"not really."

Their shoulders brush as they head down the quaint hallway. There is an absence of sound, and soft murmurs can be heard in the distance, laughter, but still, the quiet overtakes it all. Their feet pad softly against the wooden flooring, causing each step to creak. Dorothea's Inn is ancient, an old house turned inn from the late seventies.

Indie stalls in her steps. "Colleen mentioned that she saw you with a guy." Her hand catches her friend's wrist. "I was going to ask you about it a few days ago, but I know it's been weird with your mom's birthday coming up, and we haven't talked much with classes. But, is this about a guy?" She searches Nova's eyes next to her.

"Atlas," Nova finds herself correcting her. "Um, his name is Atlas. And, I don't know." She shakes her head. "Why is it so hard to be friends with people? I mean—being friends with you is easy. Being friends with anyone else has never been this hard. He's flaky. But, he's *kind*—sort of, and he listens to me talk. He doesn't interrupt me or anything. He listens to me rant about the stars."

"Gosh, a man who listens to your endless facts? Sign me up."

Nova rolls her eyes. "Shut up," she laughs.

Indie sobers. "He seems nice, Maggie. You deserve a good friend. So long as he doesn't take my place—that is."

Indie figures Nova Magnolia Hawkins deserves the world.

"Yeah, well, I can't be friends with someone who doesn't want to be friends with me, now can I? Besides, we've hung out four times or something. He seems to have his own stuff going on, you know?"

"We've all got our own stuff going on, Nova. I still have plenty of time for friends, though. That isn't an excuse if he's being rude to you or something. You're the best person that I know. Who wouldn't want to be friends with you? I can talk some sense into him if you want me to."

Snorting, Nova shakes her head. "No. No, I am definitely fine."

"I'm serious—remember those kid karate classes our moms put us in? I can kick some serious ass, Hawkins," Indie says, her arms moving in flaring motions as she karate-chops down the hall.

She kicks and twirls—her giggles filling the air. Indie Hayward-Adams is a wayward star—a shining soul filled with love.

"Okay, okay—Carmen Sandiego. We get it," Nova giggles.

Indie and Nova's mothers were best friends. After their daughters became friends at the age of four, the pair had become inseparable. Marjorie and Ines. Two stars orbiting. Ines is now missing half of her heart. So is Nova. Shared grief is haunting.

"Don't be jealous. I'm pretty awesome. But that is beside the point. The point is that—you seem to really like him, as a *friend*." Indie places quotations at the end. "And sometimes it's hard. I feel like if you just spoke to him, it would make way more sense. You might have more in common with him than you know." She shrugs.

"Yeah. Maybe," she mumbles.

The air dissipates around them as they push through the connecting doors between the inn and the diner. Sienna's mom constantly has the AC running despite the autumn temperatures falling every second. The chatter is much louder in the restaurant. Familiar faces are evident as the pair passes the booths. They sit at the same table and have since high school. Three booths down from the door, beside the window. Their corner. Their secrets and innermost fears are spoken here among the chatter and the laughter—alongside the scent of bread.

Nova lowers herself into the booth. The cushion is comforting and familiar. She clings to familiar things. Otherwise, life seems to be changing constantly, shifting before her eyes. She leans her head back against the booth and heaves heavily.

"Yeah, me too," Indie sounds from across the table.

Her hands dig into the rough fabric of her jeans. Life has become far less colorful since her mother died. Dull compared to the once vibrant, magical life her mother had once shown her.

It is weird to sit in this diner without her. Everything seems almost trivial without her mother, like the importance has weakened in her absence. Frowning, Nova runs her finger along the ridged edge of the table, picking at the peeling plastic.

"Do you know what you're going to get?" Indie asks, browsing the menu items. "I've never had the BLT here before,"

"Because you hate tomatoes," Nova responds slowly.

Indie opens her mouth to object. "Yeah, but, okay, true. But this year is all about trying new things, right? It might grow on me finally."

Nova doubts it, but she says nothing otherwise.

Humming, Indie lowers the menu. "Tell me more about this, Atlas. What is he like—is he hot?" She wiggles her brows.

"I am...*not* answering that." Nova cringes.

"Is that a yes, then?"

Nova rolls her eyes, ignoring her friend's insistent probing by glancing back at the menu. Her eyes wander mindlessly about the plastic-covered page. Across from her, Indie drums her fingers impatiently against the table, humming as she coaxes her along.

"Fine." Nova lets out an exaggerated sigh, leaning back.

There is a moment of stillness before she speaks once more.

"He's different." Softness and hesitation line her voice. "Not in a bad way, but I don't know—he found me at the park on Mom's anniversary, and we talked a bit. I needed a friend that day—"

"—Sorry," Indie interjects. "We should've been there for you."

"It's not your fault. But it was nice to talk to someone who didn't know me, who wasn't trying to make sure that I wouldn't break any second that day. He listened, sort of. He was kinda standoffish at first, but he was kind nonetheless." She shrugs.

"Good." Indie pats her hand. "That's great, Nova."

Talking with Atlas felt like falling; it felt free to speak to him.

Clearing her throat, Nova straightens. "I'm going to head to the restroom. Order for me?" she asks as she slides toward the end of the booth. "It's just my usual." She watches as Indie nods in response, waving her off. She shakes her head before turning toward the restroom.

Her footsteps seem minuscule abaft the loudness that echoes the diner. She feels minuscule, like a speck—a floating, stupid speck. Lost in a world that is too large for her to fit into. But then again, most of her life felt that way. She tightens her grip on her jacket, clutching it closer as the cool air begins to seep in. Autumn has its many perks, but the downfall will always be the growing cold. As she rounds the corner, Nova feels the familiar insistent vibration of her phone in her pocket. Pursing her lips, she cannot suppress the roll of her eyes at seeing Indie's name across the screen. She swears Indie has the memory of a squirrel.

Her fingers glide across the screen as she quickly sends the girl her order. It isn't like she doesn't order the same thing every time. Shaking her head, Nova snorts, laughing at the text coming across.

"Nova."

Her head raises at the sound of her name. At the sound of his voice. She cannot forget his voice—cannot rid herself of it even if she tries. Atlas. His name hangs to her lips, but she cannot find it within her to speak. Because her words jumble—they would.

He stands before her in a dark blue flannel, a hoodie covering it, and his signature boots. His hair is dampened from the apparent rain, and his expression is somber.

"Atlas," she forces herself to speak.

His brow raises at her breathy tone. As he leans against the wall behind him, his eyes slowly track her body, taking in the far too oversized jean jacket that adorns her shoulders—the combat boots that hang to her feet instead of Converse. Ruffled socks peeking out at the top, and her legs—bare. Her legs are bare, hardly covered by her short skirt. Atlas clears his throat, his eyes fluttering away.

"I was getting food," he explains himself despite her lack of questioning. "Saw you so, I decided to uh—say hey, I guess."

His uncertainty is amusing. "You guess?" she copies.

"I wanted to talk," he corrects, pushing off the wall. "I wanted to apologize for the other day—not showing up." Atlas shifts uncomfortably. "I had something come up. Sorry."

Nova furrows her brow. "You know, that was the worst apology anyone has ever given me." She watches his face falter. "But I think it might be the sincerest one as well. So, I guess, I accept?" She punches his shoulder awkwardly.

He winces.

She grimaces. "Sorry."

"Mhm."

Nova loosens her posture. "Well, this is awkward so, if you'd excuse me. I need to use the restroom—I'll see you around, Atlas."

"We should talk," he says as she passes.

Her steps falter. "I thought you were getting food."

"I can, after we talk."

"I'm here with a friend—Indie, so. I should get back to her," Nova speaks softly. "I'll see you around, right?" Her eyes train on the hand that grasps her wrist. "Atlas?" She tugs softly.

He drops her wrist as though it has offended him—burned him, "Sorry," he whispers. "You're right. Sorry," he repeats.

"You okay?" she asks.

"Yeah." He nods.

His eyes say otherwise. Tired, worn around the edges.

Nova chews on her lips, contemplating her next words. "I guess I can sit for a bit." Those are not the words she had in mind.

She gestures to the counter to the left of them. The wooden high seats swing as the pair sits. She shuffles, their proximity causing her to shift uncomfortably. Atlas appears to be just as at odds. She shoots him a hesitant smile, tightened—it is not received. He only averts his eyes. Nova covers her smile with a cough, her eyes darting to the right of her. His hands drum against the table.

"So, how is the weather?" she asks, wincing.

Atlas casts her a confused look, gesturing to his dampened hair.

"Right—yep."

He tilts his head. "You weren't this awkward the last time we spoke. Am I making you uncomfortable, Nova?"

Yes. "No." She nods, pausing before shaking her head.

"Right." He stifles a smirk.

There is silence.

"How have you been?"

"Fine."

"Nice," he drums his fingers against the table.

"This is weird." Nova comments after a beat.

"Conversations between strangers normally are," he murmurs.

"We're friends, remember?"

"That seems very elementary."

"Do you only answer in short sentences?"

"....yes."

She cannot contain the groan that leaves her mouth. "I hate you."

He chuckles softly, and Nova notes that it might be the most beautiful sound she has ever heard because Atlas laughs with his entire face. Crinkled eyes, a brightening smile; deep, throaty. Hidden all in the same, but when Atlas laughs and the sun comes out—it is beautiful.

"Yeah, Nova," he says once his laughter dies. "We're friends."

She hides her shock behind sarcasm. "Wow, I moved from acquaintance to friend after two weeks of not seeing each other? You must *really* like me, Atlas," Nova jokes.

"Tolerate would be a better word, but sure."

She shrugs. "I'll take what I can get."

"S'not much," he grumbles.

"That's fine." Nova can't contain her smile.

"I still don't text."

"How old are you, forty?" She snorts.

"Twenty-three," he corrects.

She pauses. "Huh."

"Problem?"

"Nope." She emphasizes the *p*.

"Mhm."

Clapping, Nova straightens. "Well, this was eventful. But I should head back"—she points over her shoulder—"to my friend. Not..." She clears her throat. "That you are not my friend because you are. Apparently. But I came here with someone, not on a date though—"

"Nova," he interrupts her rambling, amusement coating his tone.

"Yes?" She hides slightly behind her hair.

"Goodnight." He stifles a chuckle as he rises.

She flushes. "Goodnight, Atlas."

He looms over her at full height, his warmth shrouding her trembling form. Nova is not sure how, but Atlas always seems to carry warmth with him. She remembers it from their last meeting; in his proximity, warmth seemed to engulf her. She stands as well, their chests nearly touching. His chin comes above her head, and as he leans down to speak, his nose brushes against her hair. Nova tilts her head, sucking in a breath from their closeness.

"Goodnight," he repeats, his words muffling among the chatter from around them. "Goodnight—Nova." Her name tumbles from his lips.

Her fingertips brush his jacket as she brings a hand up to touch a fallen strand from her face, "Goodnight." She nods.

Though neither of them moves.

They are locked in a consistent staring competition.

"One BLT, no tomato—extra mayo, and a double Susie with no onions; hold the pickle, extra mayo with two Cherry Cokes!"

Snap. As quickly as the moment began, it has ended.

"That's my order," Nova mumbles, stepping back.

"I should head home," Atlas murmurs, moving around her.

The air seems to shift—Nova wonders if his eyes were that blue when they first met. She wonders how his nose has gained the slight crook he so confidently sports. Has his aftershave always smelled that way—she didn't notice it the last time either.

Her legs move robotically toward the counter. Her mouth manages to move upward into a smile, and her hands grip the tray. Somehow, amid her thoughts, Nova has returned to the same booth—three from the door. The cushion feels weird, different. She notices Sienna this time and watches as the woman's mouth moves—speaking to her, though she can't quite hear it well. She watches as Indie and Sienna laugh, and she forces herself to laugh along with them. But her mind is far more preoccupied.

Her mind is seeking goodnights, half-smiles, and blue eyes.

Laughs fill the air, crinkles in eyes.

Flannels, boots, greens, and grays.

Goodnight. Goodnight. Goodnight.

Friendship—companionship.

Her mind is seeking the blue, pained-filled eyes of Atlas Hale.

chapter six.
parties, midnights, and cardigans.

The pungent scent of sweat coats his nostrils; the fragrant musk clouds senses, and as Atlas fights back the bile that threatens to rise from his throat—he can't help but wonder how he has managed to place himself in this position. Bodies sway, dancing as profanity-driven music bounds from the speakers overhead. His nose upturns in disgust as he watches from across the room as Damien all but swallows the woman pressed against his chest. Her insistent giggles waft through the air—a sound that makes him want to grate nails against his eardrums to extinguish the noise. Parties have never quite been his cup of tea; it is more a torture-inducing pastime that is forced upon him by his friend. Beside him, Parker slumps against the kitchen island—his ebony hair painting across his forehead from the sweat that accumulates above his brow. A pained groan sounds from him.

"I'm going to kill him," Parker rasps. "Murder, torture, the whole

shebang," he manages to heave. "I'll make it slow."

Parker is more Damien's friend than his own. But, because of their shared friend, he's always around, much to Atlas' distaste. Curling his lip, Atlas hums in agreement as he raises his cup to his mouth. For once, he and Parker agree on something. A frown settles on his face at the thought. *Hell must be freezing over.* He shakes his head. As he pushes himself from the wall, Atlas strolls over to the distressed man, patting him as empathetically as he can manage on the back. Parker is a lightweight, always has been. He groans in response to Atlas' touch.

"You'll live," is the man's response.

An insolent '*fuck you*' is the only sound that meets his ears.

"Atlas, my man." The familiar warmth that always seems to follow Damien engulfs him. "Did you miss me, buddy?" he slurs.

In the way that people miss diseases, Atlas threatens to say.

"You're drunk." He attempts to push the man off.

"Only a tiny bit." Damien gestures with his fingers. "Just a little." Though the word comes out more as *whittle*. His breath fans his face, making the older man recoil. "I'm so happy to see you."

Damien is an emotional drunk, much to Atlas' displeasure.

"I missed you so much." His eyes begin to well with tears.

"No." Atlas pushes him away. "Nope. Stop. Seriously, I might fucking punch you if you cry, Damien."

"I can't"—*hiccup*—"help it." Damien sniffles.

"Damien." He grits his teeth. "I swear to God."

"You're my best friend. I don't know where I would—"

Atlas covers his friend's mouth. "We're leaving. Go."

Damien pouts, removing his hand. "But the party has barely even started. You're no fun, Hale," he complains.

"And now it's ending—move." He pushes him toward the door.

"You're such a party pooper, did you know that?" he objects.

"Shut up," Parker sounds from behind them.

The air shifts, and the overhaul of warmth from the mass of bodies deteriorates. The lawn is scattered with fallen solo cups and the occasional drunken sleeper; otherwise, the yard is empty, with most of the partygoers inside grinding among one another and indulging in various types of drugs.

"Atlas?" her voice is like a vise—a beacon.

She seems more than surprised to see him.

He can say the same.

His grip on his friend's shirt loosens. "Nova."

Damien perks up at the name. "Nova? You're Nova?" His hazy eyes trail the length of her body, "Huh, you know, you're much prettier than he made you out to b—*ouch*." He hisses as a stern fist connects with his abdomen. "You piece of shit! What the hell?"

Parker shrugs. "Hand slipped. Come on, it's freezing."

Atlas silently thanks the darker-haired man.

Turning his attention back to her, Atlas takes notice of the combat boots she wears—the short skirt that clings to her hips accompanied by a cerulean cardigan. It is similar to her attire the last time they had seen one another, although her hair was pulled back into a low bun now, showcasing her neck. His eyes trail the column of her neck, taking in the flush of skin against her collarbone, most likely from the cold. The colored cardigan she wears compliments her olive skin tone and accentuates the freckles that pepper her cheeks. She is serene. Truly a sight. Her chestnut hair shifts in the overhead light of the moon, shiny, opaque. She is beautiful.

Averting his eyes, Atlas clears his throat. "So, what are you doing here?" he asks, shifting uncomfortably.

"Um, Indie and Sienna are inside," Nova explains, tugging nervously at a strand of fallen hair. "It was crowded, so I came outside for air. Parties aren't exactly my thing…very stuffy. Too loud, y'know?"

He hums, nodding. He knows. He definitely knows.

"But uh, you're here," Nova bumps his shoulder. "I never expected you to have any friends outside of me," she says jokingly.

Smirking, Atlas nods toward the empty sidewalk, his footing changing directions. "Because I'm so unapproachable?"

Their shoulders brush, the tips of their fingers touching.

Raising her brow at his words, Nova takes in his hooded blue eyes, "Are you drunk right now, Atlas?" she stifles a laugh.

Shaking his head, bringing his finger to his mouth, he blows softly.

"Ah." She nods. "Makes sense."

"Explains my decent mood, huh?"

"You're not as unapproachable as you think, Hale."

"Unfortunately."

Silence hangs in the air. The further the pair goes from the party, the quieter the street becomes. Her boots crunch softly against the fallen leaves—accompanying the faint sound of scurrying animals in the wake.

"I was going to call you a few days ago," she says, breaking the silence, "but I figured that I should give it a few more days in case you decided to, y'know, change your mind again or something."

"You're hilarious. Truly," he responds dryly. "What were you going to call me about anyway?" Atlas asks, kicking a nearby rock.

"Oh." Nova shakes her head. "Nothing important. The new museum opened in town, and we haven't hung out before. I was going to ask if you wanted to check it out with me?"

"Sounds like a date," he grumbles.

"No—uh, no. I mean, not that you're like *undateable* or something. But we're friends, right? I don't want to date you. Not that someone else wouldn't want to. I mean, you're an attractive guy." Her eyes widened at her words. "No. That isn't what I meant to say, like at *all*—"

"Nova," he speaks her name softly

"Yes?" A sigh hovers among her words.

"I'll see you tomorrow."

She looks up at him, hiding behind her hair. "Really?"

"If it'll get you to stop talking, then yes."

"It'll be really fun, promise. You won't regret it."

"Somehow, I truly doubt that."

Amid their conversation, the pair circled back around to the house. The loud music has returned, as has the awkwardness. Nova shifts in place, tugging at her sleeves.

"Stop," Atlas chastises her.

"Sorry." She loosens her grip. "Habit."

"I should head out," Atlas says, his hands wound in his pockets. He nods toward the door. "Go inside."

She nods. Once, twice. Though she didn't move.

"It's nearly midnight—it's late."

"Right," Nova agrees.

His chin hovers above her head, and his hand itches to touch her. Drawing in a breath through his nose, Atlas reaches out, his movements startling her. His hand plucks a piece of lint from her shirt.

"Lint." He flicks his hand.

"Right," she repeats.

"You should try dry cleaning it."

"Duly noted."

Silence follows.

"Tomorrow?" he finds himself asking.

Her smile is small, quaint. "Tomorrow."

chapter seven.
the list, chesterfield park, and the past

Atlas notes the crinkles near her eyes when she smiles. He watches as she leans back and laughs as though he had uttered the funniest thing she's ever heard. The rasp, the shuttered giggle that tumbles from her lips, was the sound he wanted to hear forever. Atlas wonders why he had deprived himself of her company. For many weeks, he had dreaded being in her presence.

"And then," her laughter echoes, "she fell on her ass. And she somehow managed to fracture her bone—I hadn't even realized there was one to break in there." She shakes her head, wiping her hands. "She couldn't walk for months. It was hilarious, honestly."

"Your life is way more interesting than mine."

"Eh, hardly." She shrugs. "I think my friends might be funnier for sure, though. There's never a dull moment with Indie and Sienna."

He hums, leaning back against the cool booth. Doha's was a quaint bookshop down the road from the museum. The dusty smell

of books wafted in the air as the pair sat. The cramped corner houses three booths and a set of three tables—a small counter sits diagonally, occupying a coffee shop that sold baked goods. Atlas inhales deeply, his head leaning against the wall. The soft murmurs from the opposite table lulls him away. It is odd, being here with someone other than himself.

"Thank you." Her voice invades his thoughts. "I've passed by here every day, and I don't think I've ever come inside." She marvels at the large stacks of books. "It's beautiful, seriously. Thanks."

He shifts uncomfortably. "I wanted to come, anyway."

It was no big deal, he wants to say. *You like it.*

She raises her brow at his visible discomfort. "So," she opts to change the subject. "Do you have any siblings?" she asks, running a finger along the edge of her cup, "Got any weird uncles or something?"

Atlas snorts. "What is this, twenty questions?"

She shrugs. "Could be. We barely know one another. What better way to get to know someone than asking their deepest secrets?"

"*Ah yes*, the elementary school way of making friends."

She rolls her eyes, ignoring his sarcasm. "Favorite book?"

"The Goldfinch. Favorite movie?" he answers and asks, deciding to play along despite the childishness.

"Uh, Dead Poets Society?" She seems unsure.

He raises his brow, glancing up at her from beneath dark lashes.

She sighs. "It's Tangled, happy?"

He only smirks in response.

Sticking her tongue out, Nova leans forward, resting her arms against the table. "What are you drawing over there?" she questions.

The torn napkin he had snagged from the empty table beside them was covered in darkened ink—the color matched his shirt. Black woven wool. His long sleeve clung to his chest, shifting under his movements.

He pulls the napkin closer, narrowing his eyes. "Nothing."

"Lies. You've been scribbling away for fifteen minutes."

"You watchin' me or something?" Though he wasn't looking at her, his tone was amused, and a soft smirk lined his smile.

Nova sucks in a breath. "*I*...no."

The stroke of his pen sounded in the café. "Mhm."

"Whatever," she dismisses him. "So, what do your parents do?" she asks, moving on to the next question, "like for work—and stuff?"

She asks because the question was normal.

Unfortunately, his life is everything but ordinary.

The room seems to still at her words.

The silence is deafening—suffocating.

Nova glances up, confusion waning as she takes in the stormy look in his eyes—the tightening of his jaw in response to her words. His large form seems to slump in the otherwise small booth, and a look resembling something so close to defeat shrouded his face.

"Atlas?" She speaks his name with caution.

His tongue feels like it weighs a ton. How can he tell someone that he barely knows that his father is a drunken criminal, that his mother is too coked up even to realize that he exists? Will he then have to tell her about his childhood—the pain that clouds every memory? How can he tell her that he stole alcohol for his father, that his record is covered in trips to juvie because of it? His last name is more than a disgrace—it's a curse. So, instead, he pushes his drawing aside and stands, clenching his jacket in his free hand.

"Atlas?" She speaks his name again, gathering her things.

His face is stone. Tightened.

"I'm sorry," she says in a rushed tone as he turns. "I overstepped. That wasn't my intention—I'm sorry. But don't leave, all right? I won't ask about your parents again. Noted. Please don't leave."

Her desperation is borderline pathetic.

"No more questions." It isn't a request.

"No more questions," she whispers, nodding.

He swallows thickly, almost embarrassed at his outburst.

"Nova..." he begins, though she silenced him with a shake. Nova never pushes, from what he can tell. He likes that about her. He likes that she didn't force him to speak, unlike Damien.

"Come on." Nova takes in his discomfort. "We can take a walk or something. It's finally not raining for once. Besides, I think that I know a place." She beckons him toward the door. "It'll be fun," she promises.

"The park, *of course*."

"You say it like I brought you to the devil on a platter," Nova snorts. "The park is fun, and it's calm." She attempts to explain, "I feel like you could use a bit of calm after...earlier. Which I am still sorry about, by the way. I understand, though. My mom died two years ago, and bringing her up in conversation still hurts, I get it."

"Thanks," he mutters.

The leaves crunch beneath their feet as the pair walks. Above, the clouds shroud the last bit of sunlight, attempting to shine through. As they walk, embracing the silence, their hands touch, briefly, momentarily—Nova snaps her head up, clearing her throat as she tucks her hand into her pocket. She murmurs a soft apology, but Atlas doesn't seem bothered. Among the silence, Nova feels her mind beginning to rush. Questions upon questions linger on her tongue. She wishes to know so much about him. So much. Drawing a deep breath, Nova speaks the words she had been contemplating since the day she met him, "I want to show you the stars, Atlas."

"Could you be any more ominous?"

"Whatever," she shakes her head. "No, I mean—the world. I remember you saying that you couldn't understand how I saw the world in the ways that I did—so I decided to show you."

"If this is your attempt to make me *approachable*." He stifles a frown. "I hate to break it to you, Nova, but it's not going to work."

"I don't think even God himself could make you approachable."

Atlas snorts. "What do you mean?" he asks, referring to her original statement. "How does one *see* the stars?"

A smile rises to her lips at his question. "You have to hear me out," she says sternly, her face stoic. "You can't say no right away either."

"Yeah, we'll see."

Rummaging through her bag, Nova huffs, "I'm serious."

"We'll see," he repeats.

Clasping the piece of paper, Nova grins. "Found it!"

Glancing at the paper in her hand, Atlas recoils at the sight. "No."

"You don't even know what it is!"

"The answer is still no."

"Atlas, seriously."

"You should come with a warning label, Hawkins. Beware: Nova Hawkins is bound to make you want to throw yourself from a cliff."

Nova deadpans, "That is just rude."

"It's the truth," he shoots back, irritation coating his tone. "If I knew that your offer for friendship was an attempt to give me some freaking personality makeover, I would've never accepted it."

"Atlas," she attempts to interject.

"This is stupid. I'm going home."

"My mother is dead, Atlas." Her words stall his steps. "She's dead and had so many things that she wanted to do in life but never got the chance to do. Before she died, she left me this list and a letter. She said that she wanted me to see this world in the way that she had once. It took me two years to even open it. But she always painted the world perfectly, even though I know it's not. I was in the worst pain ever when I met you here that day. I miss her so much, but talking to you about life and the world—how beautiful it is—made it better."

He scowls. "Are you fucking guilt-tripping me?"

She shoots him a look at his choice of profanity.

"The point I'm trying to make is that you see the world as this terrible, horrendous place because maybe it's been unkind to you. But I think that maybe if someone showed you the beauty in life, it would be a happier place for you. And maybe it wouldn't suck so much."

"So what, she made a bucket list?"

"Essentially." She searches his eyes. "It's a list of my mom's favorite places around town. She wanted to give me something to remember her by, but I was too afraid to visit them alone. And I know that sounds stupid, and maybe it's a bit sudden, but sometimes being alone sucks, and you're not bad company."

"So you want a stranger that you've barely known for weeks to come with you to sentimental places that your mother used to visit?" he says slowly. "That's the most absurd thing I've ever heard."

"Everyone else treats me like I'm broken. Like I'll shatter to pieces at the very mention of her name. Meanwhile, you have been blatantly rude to me on various occasions, and it's nice to have someone not treat me like I might break. So yes, I want to visit them with you. I want to visit them with you because, maybe if you saw the world like she did, you wouldn't be so sad or resent the world."

There is a moment of silence.

Their eyes lock, hers pleading and his guarded.

"Please," she whispers.

He runs a rough hand down his face, a struggled groan escaping past his lips. "I don't know. I don't know, Nova. This is a lot."

"You never have to talk to me again after this. I promise we won't have to be friends after you help me with this."

"You're not *that* annoying."

Silence.

Atlas groans again. "Whatever." She let out an audible sigh of relief. "But…" He raised his hand. "This is weird, all right? This is personal to you—obviously. And sometimes, emotions can get in the way. You're obviously still hurting about your mother, so don't mistake my kindness for anything else. Don't fall in love with me or something because I'm doing this with you. You're okay, company, Nova. I like being around you, I guess. I don't want to ruin this. Whatever it is, anyway."

"No falling in love with you—got it."

"I'm being serious, Nova."

"So I am. No falling in love."

"Hawkins, I swear to God."

"Add to your list of rules. Here, we can even shake on it."

He shoots her an exasperated look.

She holds up her pinky, glancing up at him expectantly. "Promise."

She looks almost radiant in the light—like the sun somehow swallowed her whole without burning her. She looks windswept, incandescent. She looks free here. Her eyes are filled with wonder and promise. Promises that he can't seem to comprehend, alongside hope. Atlas has never been fond of hope. Hope isn't meant for people like him. But Nova, she deserves hope—all of it.

Swallowing thickly, Atlas slowly hooks his finger around her own. She smiles up at him—full lips raising from a pout. He has never wanted a friend, never wanted companionship, not until her. Not until she stumbled into his life with the grace of a tumbling child. She smiles. She speaks of the stars like they were friends. And for that reason, he wants to see her smile. He wants that smile to stay forever. He has never wanted friends, a companion—not until Nova. But here, as her eyes twinkle under the light, he wants so much. Weeks have gone by, and somehow, amid his confusing life, Nova appeared. So he nods, once, twice. He agrees to alter his life and perception of reality because Nova has hope.

"*Promise*," he utters.

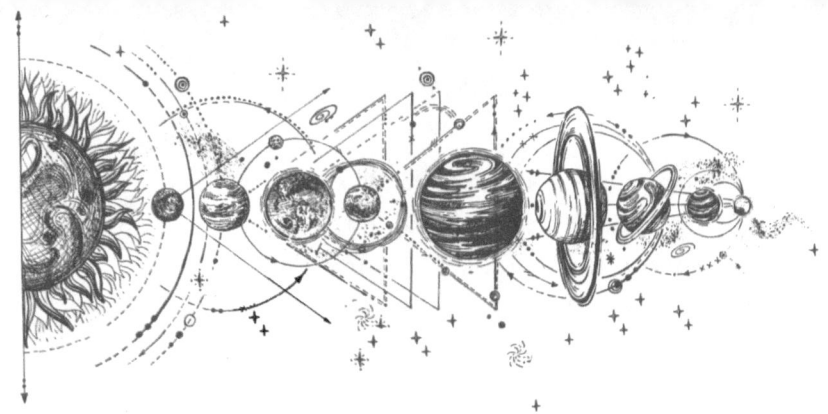

chapter eight.
who is atlas hale?

A tlas has never been fond of outings. The forced need to talk, whether in small increments to avoid seeming rude or in carried conversation that never ceased—regardless, Atlas despises the whole ordeal. So, how he has managed to find himself in this particular predicament is blurry. As he sits pressed into the edge of the narrowed couch, he feels the familiar tinge of aggravation rise. The scent of warm spice and vanilla fills the air alongside the insistent laughter that seems to echo among the group. His jaw tightens, a deepened sigh escaping past his lips as the woman he has hardly known for more than five minutes brushes against his chest, laughing loudly at something her friend said. This is not what he imagined when Nova had invited him over. Not in the slightest.

"Gosh, Indie—give the man a break. He's had a crush on you since we were in high school," the blonde to the right of him chastises her friend. "Besides, he lost the braces and the lisp. If you ignore that he

smells like bologna—he's kind of hot, honestly."

Scoffing, Indie pushes her friend softly. "Then you date him."

"Oh, no way. That's all you. No, thank you."

On the other side of the couch, Nova shoots him an apologetic smile. "Sorry," she mouths.

He responds with only a grimace.

"What about you, Nova? Have you got your eye on anyone?"

"Sienna." Indie shoots her a warning glance.

"What?" Sienna feigns innocence. "It's just a question."

Blushing, Nova shakes her head. "No comment."

"*Puh-lease*," Sienna exaggerates. "Rowan has been giving you some serious eyes lately. You, Nova girl, have an admirer."

Atlas perks up, his head turning to glance at the blushing brunette. Their eyes catch briefly. His questioning, and hers, for some reason—pleading. He raises his brow and lets his eyes travel down her face before zeroing in on the soft tug and pull at her sleeve. He frowns before coughing loudly, gaining the attention of the other two.

"Sorry." He is not sorry. "Allergies. You should dust."

Sienna leans away, scrunching her nose in disgust. "Maybe you should get that checked out or something. It sounds contagious."

"Could I get some water, actually—Nova?"

Her head snaps up. "Huh? Oh, uh, yes. Water." She stood. "You can follow me." She shifts, beckoning him toward the kitchen.

The apartment is covered with fall decor and the occasional puppy vase. The quaint building is near the east side of town, down the road from the local church. He has driven by it plenty of times in his life.

"You can sit." She points to the bar stools.

Nova chews nervously on her bottom lip as she approaches the cabinet. It is odd—having him in her home, among her things and her closest possessions. She feels naked. The atmosphere within the apartment is warm, filled with the scent of spice and vanilla. The smell calms her nerves, if only slightly.

Retrieving the glass, Nova turns toward the refrigerator. In her rushed moments, she becomes unaware of how close he stood to her.

"I'd rather stand." His words hover above her ear.

Her head inclines to glance up at him. She notes his close shave in their proximity—the lack of beard. Despite this, she still finds his stubble to look even more attractive. She blinks at her thoughts. Shaking her head, Nova pushes the cup softly into his chest and takes a small step back. Her hand curls around the glass, awaiting his retrieval. Atlas furrows his brow at her sudden movements, but he slips the glass out of her grip, regardless. She clears her throat loudly, taking one step and then another until she is far enough away from him that his warmth no longer surrounds her.

Atlas leans one hand against the fridge, his free one pushing down on the water dispenser, "You all right?" he glances over his shoulder at her. "You seem…tense." His tone is suggestive.

"M'fine." She nods, leaning her hip against the counter. "It's been a long day—work and school. It's just a lot sometimes."

"Mm," he hums in agreement.

The sound of trickling water halts.

He takes a sip, moving to stand at her side. His fingers toy with the glass in his hand. "You should tell your friends when they're bothering you." His words are unexpected. "Or I could do it for you."

Ducking her head, Nova tucks a strand of hair behind her ear, "Sienna is just nosey sometimes." Nova shrugs. "No biggie."

He leans his forearms against the counter, his biceps flexing. His jaw seems to clench at her words, though he says nothing, simply sucking his teeth before taking another sip of water. Which, to Nova, appears to be a plethora of words. She opens her mouth to speak, but her words are cut short by the soft knock on her front door.

"You should get that." Atlas glances at her.

She nods despondently. His eyes are trained on her counter. Sighing, Nova makes her way out of the kitchen, passing the living room on her way to the door. Sienna raises her brow as she passes. Nova shrugs, pulling the door open. Before her, as though he had been spoken into existence, is Rowan. His bright smile meets her surprised expression. Suddenly, her senses are engulfed by the familiar scent of bergamot and cedarwood. His embrace is sudden, tight. He squeezes her, the coolness of his skin against her own, an indication of his time outside. Nova, in return, settles into his embrace once her shock wears off.

Rowan Asher. They met through their fathers: Rowan's being the mayor and her father being his Chief Administrative Officer and closest friend. So, they are friends by default.

"How's my best girl?" His tone is soothing.

"Good. I mean, great even." She stumbles pathetically over her words. "I thought you were in Seattle until Monday."

"I got an early flight. I missed you."

Nova isn't oblivious. Ever since she magically sprouted breasts in the seventh grade, Rowan has more than once looked her over. But she assumed that the older they became in age, his attraction toward her would diminish. Unfortunately, it has not. And her father is no help in that department either. He was hell-bent on the idea that Nova and Rowan would make a *great pair*—his words exactly. The mayor's son and his daughter. A match made in political heaven. But to Nova, Rowan will always be her friend—nothing more, nothing less. Simply that.

Despite her lack of physical attraction toward the man, she cares about Rowan. So she cannot seem to contain her smile at his words. His hand cradles the back of her neck, and his eyes shine with a love that she can never return. Pressing his lips to her forehead, he hums in contentment. And for a moment, a mere second, she let her eyes flutter close, and she imagined what it would be like to be his. Unfortunately, the obnoxious throat clearing halts the thought before it could form.

The pair pulls apart, and Rowan glances at her questioningly at the sight of the man leaning against her kitchen island. Replacing his perplexed expression with his *son of the mayor* smile, Rowan makes his way over with an outstretched hand. "Rowan Zhao-Asher, I don't think we've met before," he said, tilting his head. "And you are?"

Atlas glances down at his awaiting hand, a bored, almost lazy expression hovering on his face. "Atlas," was his short response.

With a clipped laugh, Rowan lets his hand fall beside him. "I assume you're here for movie night then? Sienna never mentioned that we were going to have another person. I would've brought more pizza."

"It's fine." Atlas straightens. His six-four form towers over Rowan's mere five-nine, causing the shorter man to take a step back. "Nova and I had plans. We're going to head into town."

Nova's brow furrows in confusion.

"Number one on your list, remember?" he recalls.

Because as much as he hates himself for it, he has memorized the damn thing the second she had given it to him. It is tucked in his pocket and has been for days. The first thing on the list is to go to Margot's Café and get the stacked blueberry pancakes 'Marjorie Style.' Whatever that means. But, right now, that is better than being here.

"The list? You showed it to him," Rowan turns to face her.

"I'll be in the car," Atlas murmurs as he moves past her. "It was nice meeting you, Ryan—Sienna, Indie." He acknowledges them.

"It's Rowan," Rowan corrects, aggravation coating his tone.

Shaking loose the pack of cigarettes in his pocket, Atlas shrugs, hitting the butt against the palm of his hand. "Mhm, yeah. That's what

I said. I'll be in the car, Nova. See you later, Robert."

Indie can't seem to contain her snort. "Sorry." She stifles a laugh. "Sorry. Not funny—definitely not funny. Sorry."

Rowan ignores her. "You showed him the list?" Betrayal steeps his words. "You barely even know him. You wouldn't even let me help you with it." Rowan frowns. "I leave for a week, and you just—"

"I don't want pity. And that is all you were going to give me. I need someone who will help me face the pain head-on, not coddle me."

"I would've been there for you. You know I would've."

"Rowan." Nova shakes her head, her coat dangling from her hand, "You would've coddled me. I don't need that from you. I have to go. This is important. Can we hang out tomorrow? Or Saturday. I gotta go."

She shoots them all a smile over her shoulder before bounding out the door. She closes it softly behind her. Nova doesn't bother to lock it; she lives with Indie and she is still inside. Her breath is visible in the air. The deeper into autumn they went, the colder it becomes, and soon, she is afraid that her thin jackets and hoodies will no longer suffice. In the lot, Atlas stands leaning against the driver-side door, his hand curling around a lighter. The faint crackle and the scent of smoke fills the air. Shaking her head, Nova purses her lips as she approaches.

"Those do kill you," she repeats her words from previous conversations. "If you die, how will I ever have the chance to fall in love with you?" Her tone is teasing, "Didn't you know—my goal is to break rule number eight." She laughs at his narrowed eyes. "Kidding."

He grunts, pushing himself from the car. She stands mere inches from him—looking up at him with expectant eyes. Atlas rolls his own, haphazardly dropping the cigarette in his mouth to the ground below.

"Happy?" he questions.

She sends him a toothy grin as she digs the toe of her Converse into the ground, pressing the cigarette beneath her foot. "Delighted."

He glances down at the crushed cigarette on the ground, pursing his lips. "Foot," he says randomly, causing her to question. "Your shoe is untied. Give me your foot." He leaned against the car and patted his thigh. "I ain't got all day, Hawkins. Tie it yourself if you want. I'm trying to be a gentleman." He glances at her expectantly.

She simply frowns, confused by his request.

Growing more annoyed by the minute, Atlas groans. "Oh, for the love of God, Nova." He leans down, clasping her calf in his hand, "I don't bite," he grumbles, placing her dirtied shoe against his thigh.

She inhales deeply at his words. "I *could've...*"

His sharp glare causes her words to falter.

He tugs softly on her foot again, his abrupt movement causing her to grasp his forearm to steady herself. Atlas stiffened at her touch, his fingers pausing as he glanced up at her from beneath his lashes. He raises his brow, causing her to remove her hand slowly.

She crosses her arms, watching every twist and pull of her shoelace. "Thank you," she whispered.

He grunts once more in response.

"Done." He dropped her foot without warning

"Rude," she scolds him.

"Just get in the car, Hawkins."

He hasn't bothered to open her door. Scoffing, Nova rounded the front of the car. She tugs on the door, throwing her tote inside before climbing in. She has never been in his car before today. And frankly, Nova is not sure what she was expecting, but clean is not one of them. The truck seems void of any dirt, and for a moment, she contemplates even setting her feet on the floor mat at all. Her form is tense, and as he pulls out of the parking lot, she lets out a soft breath.

"You cold?" he asks, though his eyes never left the road.

"No," she lies, "Thank you, though."

He shoots her a sideways glance before reaching for the heating.

Her knee bounces, hitting softly against the dash. She has never been in such proximity with a man who isn't Rowan, her father, or a family member. This is odd. Uncomfortable. The silence is deafening. She huffs, reaching down to rummage through her bag for the spare book that she always keeps on hand. Nova refuses to sit in a car, with silence choking her with every inhale she takes.

"Your friend is in love with you."

Her head slams against the dash at his words.

"Ouch," she hisses.

He glances at her, amused. "You okay?" He stifles a laugh.

She shoots a glare his way. "Why would you say that?"

His hand flexes against the steering wheel. "It's true."

"Well, it's none of your business."

"Just thought you should know."

Trust me, she thinks, *I know.*

"Can you just drive? I am not talking about this with you."

He simply grunts in response.

There is a momentary silence before she speaks again.

"He's my friend," she says softly. "I care about him, but I'm not *in* love with him? He's the best—sweet. He's loyal—"

"He sounds like a Golden Retriever. Does he fetch well, too?"

"That's not funny," Nova reprimands.

"It's kind of funny," he murmurs.

"I care about him. But he's not what I want. Not that I even know what that is—I mean, I'm twenty-one, and I've never been on a date. But, he's not what I pictured when I envisioned the man I wanted forever."

"You're a bit young for forever, don't you think?"

"It's not that young. You're like forty. What's your excuse?"

His lip twitches. "You don't wanna know my baggage."

"We're friends, right?" she asks. "Have at it."

"Yeah, friends—you're not my therapist, Hawkins. You have a decent outlook on life," he cast her a tight smile as he pulled the car into park, "let's try to keep it that way. Besides, this won't work if we both think life is shit, right? Come on, we're here, and I'm starving."

The familiar bricked building that houses Margot's Café comes into view, stalling the conversation. Nova sighs, reaching for her bag. She can't help but be interested in Atlas, his life, and his thoughts. She knows only minuscule things about him—hardly even knows his favorite color. Atlas Hale is a mystery. One that she finds herself wanting to learn and solve. She wonders about his parents, childhood, and what he likes and hates. She thinks about whether he even believes in love. Is he allergic to bees or peanuts? Who is he? Who is Atlas Hale truly? Is he kind or malicious?

"Hawkins, you coming or what?"

His voice breaks her accumulation of thoughts.

Would she like the Atlas Hale she came to know?

"Yeah," she says more to herself than him, "yeah, I'm ready."

chapter nine.
pancakes marjorie style.

"I am never eating pancakes again," she groans, slumping against the cool booth behind her. Her fingers are stained with blueberry syrup, and her teeth match. Atlas stifles a laugh from across the table, cutting into his final piece of pancake. His free hand toys with a stray napkin as a smile threatens to surface on his lips. He told her that she would not be able to finish the large mound of pancakes—so, of course, Nova made it her goal to prove him wrong. And prove him wrong she did, though the consequence is her now bulging stomach and the threatening bile that seems to rise in her throat with every inhale.

"You could have stopped," Atlas shrugs, pushing his plate aside. "But, more power to you, seriously. You proved me wrong."

She shoots him a shaky thumbs up before her head connects with the table. Atlas rolls his eyes, scooting her plate to the side. Nova peeks

up at him from beneath her half-closed lids, and despite her discomfort and stuffed stomach, she cannot stifle the smile that rises to her lips.

"Thank you," her words are muffled.

"Mhm," is his short response. .

"Atlas?" Her tone is steeped in question.

He hums in response.

"Why are you helping me?" she asks. "I mean, I'm sure you have way better things to do than help me with this. But here you are."

"You aren't as terrible as you think, Nova."

She raises her brow. "Is that supposed to be an answer?"

"No, but it's about as close to the truth as you're gonna get."

Sighing, Nova leans back. "You are truly no fun."

His head leans against the window, his arms crossing in front of his chest as he takes her in. Her hair is pulled back into a ponytail, differing from her usual style. Black-rimmed glasses sit perched atop her nose, and her freckles are far more prominent in the absence of makeup. Nova looks at him curiously, her hand subconsciously coming up to wipe her lips—where his eyes seem to be trained. Atlas clears his throat and returns his gaze to the table.

"I probably look insane right now." Nova shakes her head as she reaches for a napkin. "My fingers look like a murder scene."

"You look fine," he notes her nervous fidgeting.

She runs the napkin roughly across her bottom lip. "Did I get it?"

"No, um. Here, let me." He snags the napkin from her hand slowly. "Is this—okay?" Atlas asks as he leaned forward.

Nova freezes.

"Hawkins?" Atlas probes, "You okay?"

"I think I can do it," she protests abruptly. "Thanks, though."

Nova nearly snatches the napkin from his hand in her haste. She runs her tongue along her bottom lip to dampen the surface before beginning to wipe again. She can feel his eyes tracking her movements—silently questioning her. He furrows his brow at her actions. But, if he was thinking anything, he doesn't say much at all.

"So," she begins, attempting to rid the air of the thickening uncomfortableness. "What did you mean earlier? When you said that, I didn't want to hear your baggage—what could be so bad?"

"Mm." He clicks his tongue, a low drawl sounding from his chest. "Ask another question, doll. That's a no-go."

She coughs to cover her surprise at the term of endearment. Nova isn't sure if he even noticed the change in nickname. But, from his bored expression, she assumes it had slipped out.

He leans his forearms against the table, his fingers interlacing as he watches the wheels in her head turning—burning as she searches for another question. Atlas tilts his head, shooting her a questioning look.

"I'm thinkin'." She shooes him off. "Give me a minute."

"I can hear your wheels turning," he quips, gesturing above her head in circular motions. "Oh, they might be malfunctioning."

She huffs a laugh. "Shut it." Nova smacks his hand away. "Okay. Um, how come you don't have any friends? I mean, besides Damien and Parker. You seem to not really have anyone—why is that?"

Picking at the peeling wood on the table, he furrows his brow. "Why do you still hang out with the man who is obviously in love with you? Aren't you stringing him along a bit?" he retorts.

"Rowan knows how I feel about him," Nova defends. "There has never been anything other than friendship from me. He knows that. But he can't change the way that he feels. I mean, I've tried to think of him in the way—but it just isn't what I want. I really tried to. God knows it would make my dad the happiest he's ever been, but I don't love him. Not in the ways that it counts, at least."

"Your dad?"

"He thinks that Rowan and I are a match in political heaven. In his mind, it's good for the town—the mayor's son and his daughter. He thinks that our friendship is a good foundation." Nova explains, "I think that it's stupid. I mean—he barely even speaks to me anymore. Not so much after my mom died, but he calls me once weekly to ask about my relationship with Rowan."

His jaw tightens at her words, at her saddened expression.

"No offense," Atlas starts, "but your dad seems like a dick."

She lets out a small laugh, "Tell me about it."

There is a bout of silence.

Abaft the otherwise quiet room, faint murmurs are audible. In the distance, the soft trickle of the drain pipe outside flutters in the air. The chime of the bell above the door echoes among the desolate café as it opens and closes, letting in the fall breeze with every customer. Among the silence, Nova notes, here with Atlas—it isn't so bad. The pain that seemed to cloak this building once has dissipated, if only a bit. Atlas makes it bearable. This room had once been so widely connected to her mother and her essence. Now, the memories that once racked her brain and tainted her soul are lightened. Atlas somehow does that.

"I'm not proud of my life," Atlas speaks after some time. "The things that I've done—or the life I've had up until now. Everything about it is complicated, and the last thing that I need or want is to rope someone else into it. No one deserves any of the shards from my life, so I avoid friends or romantic partners for that reason. Less of a hassle."

"Seems a bit lonely, no?"

He simply shrugs. "I like the quiet."

"I remember." A soft smile played on her lips.

"Then you can understand why being friends with you is such a hassle." She tilts her head at his words. "You never stop talking, Nova. I'm surprised you can find the time to even breathe at this point."

"Ha, ha. Hilarious. You know, I liked it better when you could hardly stand me—when you would just sit and look all despondent."

"I can still hardly stand it," he grumbles.

"Lighten up! This is meant to be fun."

"Ah yes, the highlight of my life has been watching you scarf down a jumbo stack of pancakes so fast that it would put a sumo wrestler to shame. Seriously, my life has been made, Nova." He claps unenthusiastically. "I can die a peaceful death, alas."

Nova rolls her eyes. "Shut up."

He shakes his head, laughing softly to himself.

"What's next on the list?" he asks once he sobers.

"Um, the Willow tree, I think?"

"Am I even supposed to know what that means?"

"The Willow tree in the town square—my mom used to take me to it when I was about eight or so? There used to be a rope swing attached to it," she finds herself droning on. "Anyway, um—she carved our names into it when I was younger, and I haven't been back to it since." She runs her finger along the edge of the table, frowning. "Maybe we can skip that one. I don't um, we can do the third one instead this time."

"You don't have to explain," Atlas offers. "I get it."

Nova likes that he doesn't ask questions.

"The third task is..." He rustles through his pocket for the paper. "Uh, Betty's Bakeshop? Isn't that the weird lady over on third?"

"She isn't weird," Nova scoffs. "Betty is sweet, a bit bubbly, but sweet, and besides, her cupcakes are to die for. We can do that one next."

"You just ate five pancakes, Nova," Atlas marvels, watching as she slid to the end of the booth. "You're joking, right?"

Nova says impatiently, "Come on. We're losing daylight."

"You're so weird. Did you know that?"

"Get in the car, Hale," she repeats his earlier words.

"And bossy too," he says.

She placed her hands on the small of his back, pushing him toward the door. Nova groans, "Ugh, you weigh a ton." She huffs a breath and maneuvers her stance, "Jesus, move, you freaking mountain man." He simply chuckles in response. "Atlas," she whines.

"Do you hear that?" He cups his ear. "It's this whiny and annoying voice. It's quite grating, if I'm being honest."

Nova gapes, smacking his back. "That is rude."

"Oh no," he gasps. "It speaks again."

She giggles. "Move it, old man."

His smile is bright. Far brighter than she has ever seen it. He looks good in this way—smiling, happy. Happiness looks good on Atlas Hale. The overhead light causes his eyes to sparkle alongside the amusement that seems to cloud the very irises. She bumps shoulders with him, their steps falling in sync. Nova notes that moments with Atlas seem to be covered in whimsy, coated in laughter. His friendship, though new, somehow brings her a sense of happiness and peace.

"Thank you," she says softly.

He doesn't ask what for because he knows.

Her eyes fill with sincerity and gratitude.

"Thank you so much."

He doesn't have to ask—because Atlas knows.

Because her eyes shrouded—darkened the second they stepped into the quaint café. Because her voice trembled as she stumbled over her words to order, because she spoke so frequently of her mother, of their time there. Because pain is a lonesome friend of hers.

So he speaks no words. He doesn't need to.

He nods. Once and again, his hand brushes against her own as they continue their walk. He speaks no words because he knows.

They share pain and grief. Two souls likened.

Atlas knows.

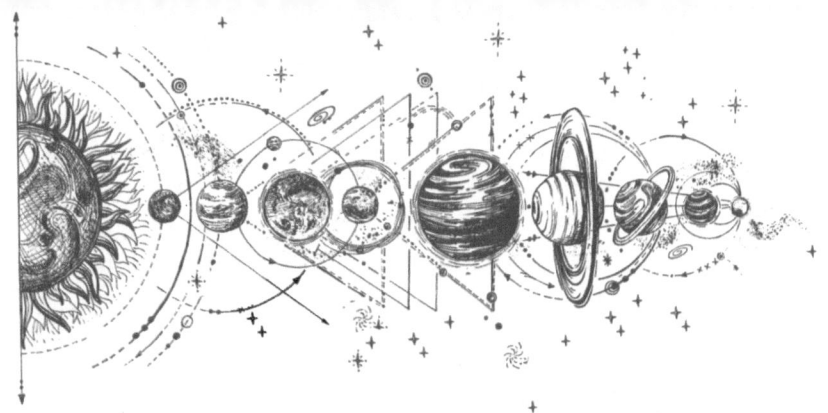

chapter ten.
Murrays convenience store part two and stargazing

Atlas watches with nervous eyes as Murray speaks animatedly to the brunette. Her eyes are filled with wonder and awe at the older man's words. She glances at Atlas occasionally, questions swimming beneath her irises, but Nova never pries—he likes that most about her. The plastic basket in his hand rocks back and forth—back and forth in communion with his body. He teeters on the balls of his feet, biting back the exasperated groan that threatens to leave his mouth. Murray is a talker. He hardly thinks much before he speaks, and the mischievous look in his eye is enough for Atlas to curse himself for even bringing her here. After their late-night escapades to the café and their attempt to visit the bakeshop across town, Nova opted for a candy break. To which he stupidly brought her to the convenience store. From what he can remember, Murray is not meant to be here, but instead, his stoner grandson Rodney is supposed to work the cash register.

He was wrong—unfortunately.

Inhaling deeply, Atlas clears his throat loudly, gaining the pair's attention. Nova looks at him sheepishly, tucking a stray hair behind her ear. Murray, well, he is an asshole whose smirk stretches across the majority of his face, and his eyes are questioning.

"I think we're talkin' a bit much." Murray's lip twitches. "Atlas tends to get bored really quickly—got the attention span of a rat. I remember one time when he was younger, he *would*—" An obnoxious cough halts his words, "—Well, I figure I should let him tell you that one." He pats her hand affectionately. "Let me get y'all rung up."

Atlas is tempted to trip the older man as he passes.

Placing the basket on the counter, Atlas clenches his jaw. "Nova, would you mind getting a water real quick? I forgot it."

She furrows her brow. "Uh, yeah sure."

It isn't until she leaves again that Atlas speaks.

"Murray, what the hell?" he hisses.

The older man raises his brow at his choice of words, the insistent beep of the cash register fueling the air. "I've known you since you were seven, and I've got the pictures to prove it. Don't make me embarrass you in front of your lady friend, boy. You might be twenty-three now, but don't you start forgetting yourself. Do I make myself clear?"

Atlas sighs, casting his gaze downward. "Sorry," he murmurs.

"You wanna try that again?"

"What did you tell her?" Atlas presses.

"Nothing worth you causing this big of a fit over, that's for sure. I wouldn't do that to you, and you should know that by now, Atlas."

Atlas. Not bud or rocket. Not even ninny. Atlas.

"You're upset with me." He furrows his brow. "Why?"

"When have I ever done anything to hurt you?" Murray asks, handing the confused man his bag. "No need to think. The answer is never. I know the life you've lived—and I know you're not proud of it. I wouldn't go around blabbing about it to a girl you obviously like."

"I don't"—he leans in—"*like* her. She's a friend. That's all."

"So was Martha once, and look at what happened to us."

Murray becomes solemn at the mention of his late wife.

Martha and Murray were married for fifty-seven years. His all but adopted parents had met in this exact store—behind the chip aisle, as Murray so frequently reminds him. One look at her and her rosy cheeks, and Murray was hooked. They became instant friends, going on movie dates to the old cinema in town—though it was now abandoned—one day, the friendship turned into something far more.

"This isn't the same thing." Atlas shakes his head.

"Does she know that?" Murray nods toward the short brunette carrying five different bottles of water. "*Hell*, do you? She looks at you like you put the moon in the sky, kiddo. That ain't just friendship."

Pursing his lips, Atlas sends him a bored expression. "Nova looks at trees that way, Murray—I'm not special. She looked at you like that."

"Maybe not to other people, but to her, you are. Even if she can't see it yet. Besides, when have you ever brought someone to meet me?"

"She was hungry," Atlas grumbles.

"The closest all-nighter is halfway across town. Try again."

"They never have the vanilla soda."

"All I'm hearin' is excuses, kid."

"She's better off without me," Atlas snaps. He looks skittish, torn, and bound to a perpetual, never-ending turmoil. "Hell, everyone is. She can't feel anything for me because I have nothing to offer her. So, for once in your life, Murray, can you *drop* it?"

"I bought like five bottles. I wasn't sure which one you wanted. I'm really picky about my waters, so—uh, which one?" Nova sounds, interrupting their heated back and forth. Taking in the thickening air surrounding the pair, Nova shifts. "Am I...interrupting something?"

"No," Atlas grabs the closest water to him, swiping it across the scale. "Come on." He shoots Murray a haunted glance. "Let's go."

Nova opens her mouth object, but the look on his face is enough to quiet her. She nods, chewing nervously on her bottom lip. "It was really nice meeting you, Mr. Murray. We should talk again soon."

"Atlas swings by every Sunday. I'm sure if you ask him, he would bring you with him. I've got a shuffleboard set up out back. There's that dinner this weekend, too, over at the Hawthorne's. You should come."

The excitement in her eyes is enough for Atlas to nod despite his bubbling annoyance. "Yeah, whatever, we'll see."

That is enough to fuel her good mood until the pair trudges back to the truck. It isn't until they are about halfway down the road, and the car begins to drown from the haunting and thickening silence, that Nova speaks again. "Did I do something?" she asks quietly.

His grip tightens against the steering wheel. "No."

She furrows her brow. "Seriously? Because I feel like I did something. You seem...*tense*. Did something happen with Murray?"

"No." He roughly shakes his head. "Everything's fine."

She glances at him wearily before sighing. "Okay."

Resting her chin against her palm, Nova leans her head against the window, watching as the condensation arose on the glass. She hums softly to herself, the tip of her finger running along, creating shapes and smiles in the window. "My mom used to do this with me. When it was cold—and the windows would fog up, we would sit inside the car and draw on the windows. It seems dumb now, but as a kid, it was always so fun. Sometimes, she would get Indie and Sienna and sit in the car for hours just listening to music and drawing on the windows."

The silence is nearly deafening.

She drags out a breath after her confession, tugging softly against her sleeves. "It's getting cold," she breaks the silence. As she reaches for the AC controls, she misses his movements, the dismissal causing their hands to brush. "Sorry," she rushes out, snatching her hand away. Her head dips as she tucked her hands under her thighs.

"Here." His arm reaches into the back seat. "Extra warmth."

A wool blanket falls into her lap.

"Thanks," she whispers.

The silence returns.

"I had fun tonight," Nova admits into the darkness.

He merely grunts in agreement.

The car shifts, the familiar groove indicating that the pair were nearing Nova's home. Funnily enough, she finds herself not wanting the night to end. She peeks over at him gnawing on her bottom lip.

"Could you pull over?"

He sends her a perplexed look. "*What*—like now?"

"Yes, I want to show you something." She straightens, clutching the blanket in her hands. "Just pull over, right here. Please."

The truck wobbles. The sudden shift in terrain caused dirt to kick up against the sides. He skids to an abrupt stop, causing the car behind them to honk their horn in annoyance. She swears she hears a string of curse words from the driver. Her hand splays against the dash as she steadies herself with a huff. Atlas simply looks at her expectantly.

"What?" He shrugs. "You wanted me to pull over."

"Yeah, pull over—*safely*. Not practically cause an accident."

He sends her a bored expression. "You're alive, aren't you?"

Huffing a breath, Nova tugs her hair from her face. "Just get out of the truck, Atlas," she grumbles, pushing her door open.

Pushing the door open, he mutters a string of curses as he slides out of the truck, slamming the door behind him. She watches with confused eyes as he rounds the front of the truck, a scowl gracing his face. His glare is far colder than the abrasive wind. Atlas grasps the passenger side door, holding out impatiently to help her down. When she takes her time grabbing it, he shoots her an exasperated look.

"Thanks," she mumbles, sliding down.

"Mhm." He gives her a once over.

"Can you let down the back—please?"

Atlas shoots her a questioning glance but pulls at the latch, nonetheless. "The last time I did this with a girl, it didn't end how I think you're hoping it will, Hawkins. You should tread very lightly."

She furrows her brow, glancing at the truck bed and back to him before a shadowed look of disgust covers her face. "You're disgusting. Help me lay this out, and do me a favor, stop speaking."

His chuckle is deep; a cloud of mist surrounding his laugh.

The truck is raised, and despite her slight jump, the brunette cannot propel herself onto the bed. She huffs, attempting again.

Atlas lets out a loud breath.

"Oh, I'm *sorry*," Nova sneers, "am I bothering you?"

"Yes, actually. It's late—I'm tired. We'll be here all night waiting for you to get on." His hands catch her waist, causing her to stumble slightly. "Stop moving. I'm just trying to help."

She sucks in a breath at his sudden movements.

"You okay?" His tone is mocking, and amusement waned.

"Yes," she finds herself saying.

"Mhm." His knees bend, and his grip tightens as he places her onto the truck bed. "You seem nervous." The pair are now the same height, though he hovers over her by an inch. "You could thank me—nod at least. You look like you're having an aneurysm."

His hands are firm against her waist, warm. She swallows thickly, her pupils enlarging as her eyes zero in on his lips.

"Thank you," she finds herself blurting out.

He smirks. "Ah, now was that so hard?"

His hands are gone, and with them with his warmth.

The truck dips, shifting and groaning under his weight.

Silence fills the air.

"You blush easily. Did you know that?"

"It's cold—that's all."

"Sure." He drags the word out.

"That's hardly the reason we're here."

"Why exactly are we here, anyway?"

"Number twelve—late-night stargazing," Nova reminds him. "It's one of the things that I looked forward to the most on the list. Out of all twenty-five of them—that one is the least heavy. The rest make me feel like I might drown if I look at them again. So this one it is."

Atlas watches as she leaned back, her hair falling around her. She lays against the cool truck bed, her hands pressing tautly against her abdomen. There is a slight smile of contentment on her face, and for a moment, a mere second—she looks almost childlike in her peace. Like the world around her could not harm, never touch her. Nova cracks an eye, a soft giggle escaping past her lips as she beckons him to lay beside her. Among the stiffening evening air and the darkened skies, Atlas feels the familiar bout of peace that seems to occur in Nova's presence. The one thing that drew him to her that first night was her ability to cause everything around her to anchor to the moon.

"She sent me a letter about two weeks after she passed."

His head turns at her words.

"You can imagine the shock that I felt when I opened my mailbox and saw a box with a letter attached to it addressed to me from my mother. I thought maybe someone was playing a prank on me, indulging in my grief, but sure enough, it was from her. Her death is something that has never made sense to me and will forever haunt me. How could someone so beautiful, kind, and carefree be fated to such a demise? But I guess maybe the glass is always half empty, dirtied, and hard to see." She swallows harshly. "I wish I had done something sooner."

"It isn't your fault—you have to know that."

"Maybe. But I should've tried harder. Gotten her to fight it."

His mouth presses closed at her words, and he contemplates briefly before speaking again. "What did the letter say?"

"She wanted me to"—she let out a tear-coated laugh—"see the world. Live the life that was unkind to her. How morbid. Life was supposed to be beautiful, but not enough to make her better."

"My mom left—for different reasons, but she left. Every day, I wonder if maybe it was my fault—if maybe I could've done something to make her stay or want me more. But she left. I live with it every day, the choices that she made. I live with it, and I am filled with grief. But sometimes, we're dealt the shit end of the stick, and as much as we wish we could escape, we have to learn to live with it, eventually."

"What if I don't know how to—live with it, I mean?"

"Then you fall victim to life and die before you've even lived. You can't hold on to it. It might not kill you in a literal sense, but eventually you'll wake up, and days will have become weeks; weeks will have become years, and life will have moved on past your grief."

Nova pushes herself up on her elbows, her head canting to the side. In her movements, her hair falls limply at her shoulders. "You sound like you're speaking from experience." She gauges his reaction.

Atlas sucks his teeth, his hands flexing as he shrugs.

"How old were you when she left?" Nova asks.

"Too young," he scoffs. "I think I was about seven or eight."

Her face pinches at his words. She opens her mouth to respond, but he merely shakes his head. Words are pointless, useless.

"Tell me about the stars," Atlas whispers. His words are pleading and steeped in pain, "Number twelve, remember?"

"What do you want to know?"

She will tell him anything—do anything. She wishes to steal his pain, extinguish his suffering if only for a moment. Atlas Hale wears his pain akin to a second skin. He is covered in it. He carries it.

"Anything."

She contemplates for a moment before speaking again.

"Have you ever heard of Perseus and Andromeda?" He shakes his head slowly. "Well then." She settles back down against the metal beside him. "You are definitely in for a beautiful story, that's for sure."

Among the darkening skies and the looming stars, Nova speaks of the love charted abaft the clouds. She tells of Perseus and Andromeda, lovers—fated and written in the stars above. She speaks animatedly as though they were friends rather than celestial entities. Her hair fans out around her, rough tendrils floating across his face, but Atlas can't find it within him to care much. In this pain, in his brokenness, for once, there is a reprieve. For once, someone looks at him without seeing his fractures. He is covered in casts, filled with wounds that cannot be healed. No matter how much he tries, his past is haunting.

But for once, for a second—someone sees him.

She sees him.

And nothing in this world has ever terrified him more.

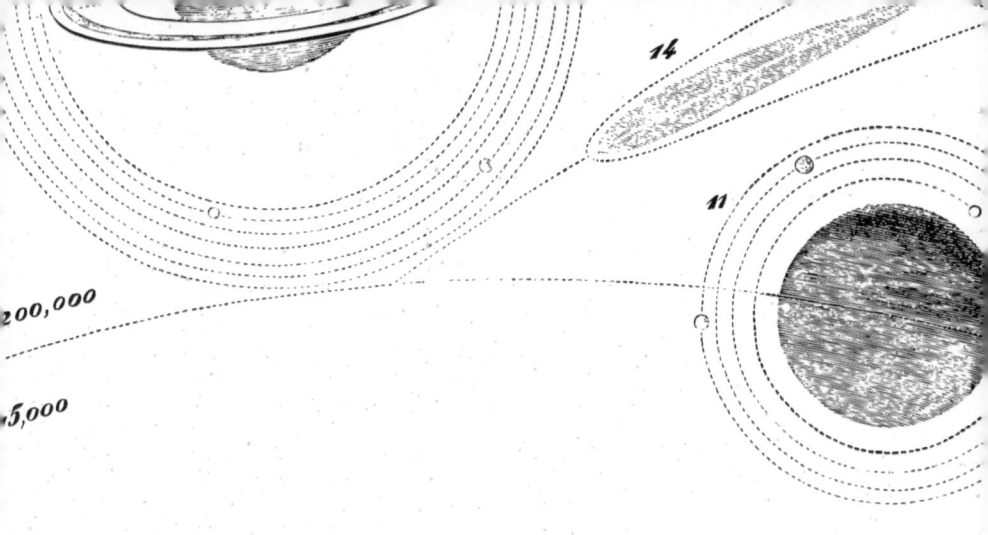

INTERLUDE.
this is atlas hale

Atlas Hale wears his melancholy akin to a second skin; he is clothed in it. Each step seems tethered to an overarching cloud of darkness that cloaks his very form. His pain drenches him and shrouds him in resemblance to a looming thunderstorm. The man carries his pain as though it is a wayward drug—symbolic of a death-inducing lifeline. He is welded to his trepidation in a shattered display of union that he cannot divorce nor rid himself of entirely.

This is Atlas Hale. This is who he was.
And Nova, well, she has always been fond of thunderstorms.

chapter eleven.
home, moments, and realizations.

Faint chatter can be heard in the distance alongside murmurs and soft laughter that fuel the surrounding air. Beneath the autumn skies, there is slight communion. Something peaceful lingers here in the wake of sunset. Atlas has stayed true to his words to Murray—the backyard of the Hawthorne family home is slightly crowded from the vast number of people accompanying it. The weekly family dinner is a staple between him and his friends. The group tucks themselves into the backyard among the long table perched in the center. She is the first outside of their small family ever to be here—it feels different with Nova.

"Your friends seem nice." Her voice meets his ears. She places a warm cup of tea into his hands as she sits. "Parker is, uh." *Distracting, loud?* "Unique. That's for sure." She smiles beneath the lip of her cup.

"Yeah, he's a character, that one," Atlas murmurs.

"This is pretty." Nova let her eyes wander the setup.

The fence is lined with lights, with some connecting across the trees; a large canopy covers the table—and a few stray chairs linger about. Beneath the darkening skies, the lights illuminate the space.

"How often do you guys do this?"

"Once a week. Mom likes to check in—see her boys," Damien answers her question. "I can take that." He gestures to her now empty cup. "I think my mom asked for you down by the tables."

"Oh, uh, sure," Nova says as she stands. "Um, I'll be back." She catches Atlas' eye and fights back the threatening blush to her cheeks. "Uh…" She flicks her thumb toward the steps. "Yeah. I'm gonna…"

Damien waits until her fleeting form disappears before he blows a low whistle, shaking his head. "She's something. Cute face."

Atlas leaned his elbows against his knees. "Subtle," he remarks with a slight smirk as Damien settles in Nova's place. "What do you want?" *Besides to lecture me*, he thinks. *And pick my brain.*

Damien sniffs. "Nothin' just wanted to talk."

Atlas casts him a look over his shoulder.

"Fine—what's up with the girl? You fuckin' her or somethin'?"

Heaving a breath, Atlas shakes his head. "I'm not having this conversation with you right now, Dame. It's been a good night."

Damien holds his hands up in surrender. "Pipe down, chump." He bumps his shoulder. "It's just a question. I was surprised, that's all. You don't normally bring girls around—not to meet Mom, at least. I was just wondering. I remembered her a bit from the party a few weeks ago."

Atlas snorts. "Surprised you remember anything with how wasted you were that night. You cried last time I checked."

Damien pulls a face. "Whatever. Besides the point entirely, I was just checking in, that's all. She's sweet, really nice."

"Shouldn't the *'hurt them and you die'* speech go to her?"

"No speech, just an observation." Damien picks at a stray piece of grass. "She fits in good here." He watches as the brunette laughs alongside his mother. "Mom likes her. That's a first for sure."

Catie Hawthorne was a beacon of light in Atlas' otherwise haunted life. When his mother had been nowhere to be found—absent, all but deserting him—Catie had been there. She had wiped his tears, fed him when his father was far too drunk to care, and gave him a room. Catie Hawthorne was his mother in all the ways that mattered. Damien was his best friend—his brother, albeit not by blood, but he was family. Sometimes, family was far more than blood. Far more than titles.

"Mom likes everyone," Atlas mumbles, before sipping his tea. "She liked me, remember? Surely, her perception's off."

Damien merely shakes his head.

Atlas leans back against the patio steps, taking in the smiling face of Nova Hawkins. Her head is thrown back; her laughter echoes out among the chatter. Her soft pink dress catches in the wind, and loose curls flutter, framing her face. She looks radiant. But then again, she always did. A soft smile settles on her face. She had the kind of smile that left you breathless, filled with an immeasurable amount of empathy and kindness—so much understanding lay beneath her eyes. Swallowing thickly, Atlas ran a tired hand through his hair as he moved to stand.

"I need a drink. You want one?" he asks.

Damien shoots him a weary look. "You good?"

"Yeah, 'm fine," he mumbles on his way down the steps.

The yard is littered with people as he crosses to the drink table. Some are on loose blankets, others in lawn chairs. Micah is sitting on the ground, Adela, his three-year-old daughter, perched on his lap while Avani tickles her stomach. Murray and Parker are caught in another heated debate—as usual. Atlas assumes Parker hardly made any sense, but when does he ever? As loud and random as ever, this is his family.

This is home.

"Oh, there he is." Catie grins. "We were just talking about you." The woman casts him a knowing glance. "Nova was telling me how she met Murray the other day. She's about as sweet as a peach."

Before Catie Hawthorne married Greg Hawthorne, she was Catie Sinclair. She resided in a small town in Tennessee before relocating to Washington for college, where she met Atlas' mother. The pair hit it off immediately. They were as thick as thieves before his mother's addiction overcame her life. Catie Sinclair has a heart of gold that only grew larger the older she became. She is his mom and has been from the moment he turned ten. Despite his upbringing and track record—Catie sees him. "Hey, Mama." He presses a kiss to her forehead. "Got any beer?"

Catie pats his cheek affectionately. "Nope. But we have sodas."

Atlas grimaces. "I'll take a water."

Nova stifles a smile as she catches his eye. He merely smirks.

"I was just about to—*Park Chen*! Take one more bite of those turnovers, and I'll hand your ass to you, I swear," Catie's warning rings out. Huffing, she brushes a piece of hair from her face. "Be a dear and help Nova finish setting the table, would you, Atlas? I'll be back."

Curses are audible in her wake.

Nova covers her mouth, chuckling to herself. Atlas shakes his head, moving to stand at her side. In his movements, their hands brush—the familiar warmth traveling up his arm, circling his heart.

"Sorry," he murmurs, moving his hand.

She glances at him sideways before tucking her chin. "S'okay."

He silently passes her a fork.

"Are you having fun?" He winces at his question.

"A lot, actually." Nova nods. "Everyone has been welcoming. Mrs. Hawthorne is lovely—really bubbly. She reminds me a lot of my mother, funnily enough." A small smile appears on her face. "You have great friends." Her eyes wandered to the group. "Adela is adorable. Seriously—I've never seen a cuter kid."

Atlas follows her gaze. "Yeah." The child's laughter fills the air, "When she's not screaming, she's a pretty sweet kid."

"How did you all meet?" she asks, handing him a plate.

The setting sun casts a shadow against his face—highlighting his deepening look of contemplation. "Damien and I met in grade school. I was"—Atlas huffs a laugh—"surprisingly getting beat up. I was a chump back then. Anyway, he stood up for me. After that, we just became attached at the hip. It helped that our moms had been friends at one point or the other. It was probably bound to happen."

Nova snorts. "I can't imagine someone beating you up."

"No?" He raises his brow, his mouth twitching.

Her eyes trail over his face before dipping down the column of his neck; his collar was ruffled slightly, matching his messy hair. He's wearing a dark brown long sleeve that clings to his chest. With his movements, the shirt rises, revealing a patch of darkened hair trailing his stomach. She coughs, averting her eyes. "No. Definitely not."

"Well, I appreciate the confidence." He smirks. "Parker came into the picture about a few years later—met him through Dame. They worked together down at Harry's. Micah, I met two years ago?" Atlas nods, confirming to himself. "He was at the park with Delly. The rest is too long of a story to tell. We all kind of stumbled across one another."

"Very eventful life you've lived, Atlas Hale."

"*Riveting*, honestly. You should be jealous."

She shakes her head at his words, laughing softly. Her grin is wide, toothy—so very Nova that, for a moment, he forgets that they aren't alone. They're too exposed here, not in the back of his truck or at the diner. They are strangers here among his friends.

"Is it odd that I wish we were alone?" The words break the air before he can even halt them. Stupid. The words are silly, but he can't help but think of them, anyway. "Sorry," he exhales. "Sorry. That's weird."

"No. Not really. It feels like we haven't spoken much today. I get it. I like talking to you, too. It feels very crowded here."

"Yeah," he agrees. His response is so low she barely heard it.

When Nova glances up at him, he feels like he's the only person there. Like the others don't matter; for once, someone only sees him.

"Thanks for coming." His eyes lock with her own.

"Thanks for inviting me," she says.

They stare at one another for what seems like hours. Like years have pass in their haze as the world halts to a standstill. Just the two of them—though, that is how it always feels when they are with one another. Like their problems have no sway or power here.

Though Adela's squeal is enough to break it.

Nova breaks first, scrambling with the napkins. "I should finish with these." She waves them. "I'll see you in a bit?"

"Yeah." He nods. "Yeah. I should, um—grab more drinks."

"Right." she agrees, though her feet are anchored to the ground.

"Right," he repeats.

Neither move nor breathe.

They are so close to one another that Nova can feel his body heat— that familiar warmth. The Atlas warmth that travels wherever he goes. He is so warm and inviting. She swallows hard, becoming far too aware of their proximity. Her head reaches slightly above his chest, though she still looms below his chin. His hand itches, aching to touch her. Remnants of the days prior on the back of his truck falter in his mind with the grace of a stumbling child. He can't forget his hands on her waist, her hair brushing against his neck. Something changed that day. Something shifted in her darkening gaze, in her fluttering stares.

This is different. Far different than he had ever wished.

He wants to kiss her. He wants to touch her, devour her.

A pain-filled groan tethered to his lips. "You should finish setting up. I need to help Parker with the grill before he lights himself on fire."

His retreating steps are nearly robotic, and he hardly waits to hear her response before he saunters away. The further from her, the looser the pain in his chest becomes. As he nears the grill, Atlas releases a breath he doesn't realize he's been holding in—it stumbles from his mouth.

This isn't going to work.

"Atlas." Micah catches his hardened gaze. "You okay?"

No, he wants to say, *this is not okay. I'm not okay.* But instead, he sends the man a curt nod and continues his march toward the house.

He passes Damien on the steps. The man looks at him oddly—questioning him, but he keeps walking. He keeps walking until the cool air breaks with the warmth surrounding the home, until his hands splay against the kitchen counter, gripping the sides, and his head is hung low. He shakes his head. A groan escapes his lips.

"Fuck," he curses. "Ah hell." He groans.

"Atlas?" Damien crowds his space.

"Fuck."

"Dude, you good?"

No, he tugs at the ends of his hair. *Far from it*, he wants to say.

"I fucked up," he whispers in horror.

Damien grips his shoulders. "Hey, look at me. What's going on?" He searches his face. "You in trouble with someone? What's happening?"

Her laugh pierces through the air, and he thinks he might puke. "Fuck."

Damien blinks. Once and again before, a Cheshire smile appears slowly on his face. He ruffles his friend's hair, his free hand clapping him on the back. "Oh, you fucker. You're so screwed." He laughs.

Screwed, Atlas thinks, *is the biggest understatement ever.*

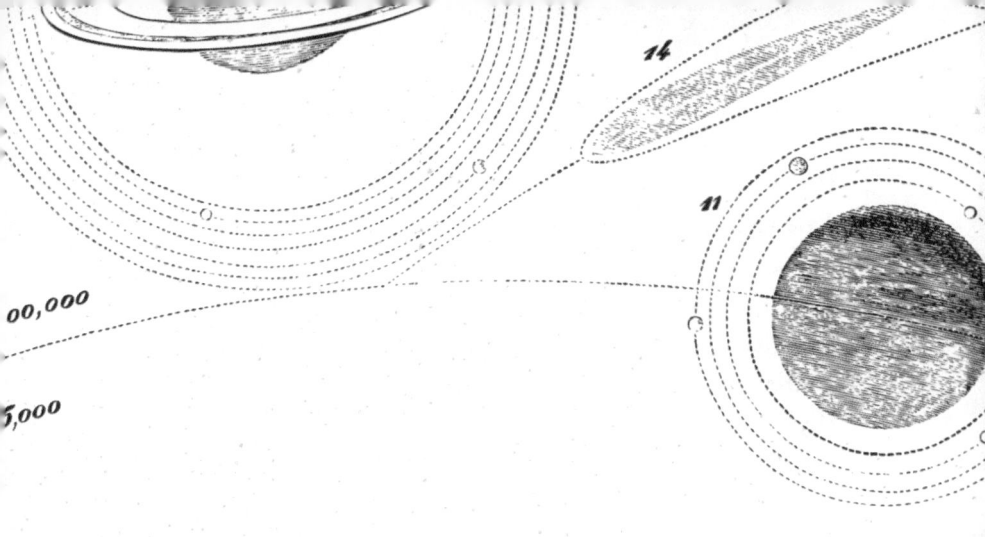

INTERLUDE.

When Nova was younger, her mother had told her that there was an *art* to falling in love: a vast intricacy. She explained that falling in love was an art form that required patience, vulnerability, and a willingness to be swept away by an all-encompassing emotion. Her mother said it was like standing on the edge of a cliff, unsure if you were ready to take the leap but knowing that the rush would be terrifying and *exhilarating*. She said it would start with a spark, a glimmer of hope that ignited in the depths of your soul; you would feel it growing, expanding, until it consumed you entirely. And that your thoughts would be consumed by the person who had captured your heart, and that you would find yourself daydreaming about them at every opportunity—every waking moment.

The art of falling in love is in the little moments, the stolen glances, the gentle touch of a hand. It's in how your heart flutters when you hear their voice and how their laughter fills you with a warmth that spreads through your entire being. It requires vulnerability, the courage to open yourself up entirely to another person, knowing they have the power to break your heart, but trusting that they won't. Falling in love is a leap of faith, a journey into the unknown without guarantees of what may lie ahead.

But despite the risks, falling in love is one of the most beautiful experiences that life has ever had to offer. It's a journey that will test, challenge, and change you in ways you never thought possible. And if you're lucky enough to find someone who loves you back, the art of falling in love becomes a *masterpiece*, an expression of the deepest and purest form of human connection. And Nova, well, she wishes for nothing more. She craves it. She craves love in its simplest form.

chapter twelve.
the boy named pluto, and moments.

Sometimes, Nova thinks that Atlas reminds her of Pluto. Whimsical, filled with ice and dust, a bit misunderstood, but Pluto—Atlas—is far larger than he seems. When she was younger, hardly old enough to sleep without a night light on, Nova remembers her mother telling her a bedtime story about the *planet left behind*—that was what Marjorie had called Pluto—she spoke of how small the planet was, *insignificant* compared to others but, for some reason, it stuck out.

Atlas Hale reminds Nova of Pluto—misunderstood, a bit cold, sort of icy, but even in his insignificance, he stands out among others. Perhaps that is why he seems to be a constant thought in her mind, even now, as she sits among the crowd in *Connies*, listening to her friend's boisterous laughter and hearty snorts. Among the fallen leaves and the soft patter of rain, Nova thinks only of him. About his smile, the quaint smile he showed around his family and friends, about the gentle

furrow in his brow that appeared so suddenly toward the night's end. She thinks about his hand, tethered to his side, twitching—*how she wished* he would reach out and hold her own.

Nova found herself wishing these past few days. She hopes for longer moments beneath his haunted gaze, wishing for anything that would tie her to him. In the time it took to close the gate to the Hawthorne's backyard that night and in the steps that followed toward her car, Nova felt the sudden change. She felt the shudder of her heart in her chest and an ache that traveled up her spine. Somewhere, amid the car ride back to her apartment, in her steps up the stairs, and in the moments it took for her to remove her coat—Nova realized that she misses him.

She *misses* Atlas.

She paused at the thought, dismissing it, and slipped her shoes off. Somewhere, in the minutes it had taken for her to close her bedroom door, she realized she liked the sound of his laughter. Somewhere, among the heavy steam of her midnight shower, Nova realized that his cologne still lingered in strands of her hair. Notes of tonka bean and clary sage clouding her senses with every circular motion.

It wasn't until her duvet surrounded her body. The lights dimmed within her room alongside the soft murmurs from her sound machine that fueled the air. Nova realized a series of very complicated facts: the first being that she feels something for Atlas Hale—the second that it was far more profound than the bucket list, far deeper than the friendship and fated laughter. It was deeper than trips to Margot's and walks in Chesterfield Park. She feels something. The third had been that she still has his jacket, and the fourth—that she had broken the one promise she had made him to him.

"*Don't fall in love with me,*" he had said.

"*Promise,*" she had uttered.

Though it wasn't love, not at all, not really, but it was *something*.

It was something far more than she had ever meant to feel.

"*Promise,*" he had replied.

Sometimes, Nova thinks that Atlas reminds her of Pluto. Whimsical, filled with ice and dust a bit misunderstood, but Pluto—Atlas—is far larger than he seems. Small, insignificant to most, but to Nova, Atlas Hale is the largest planet ever to grace her galaxy.

Only sometimes, when the moon hangs low and the darkness creeps in—Nova thinks Atlas reminded her of Pluto.

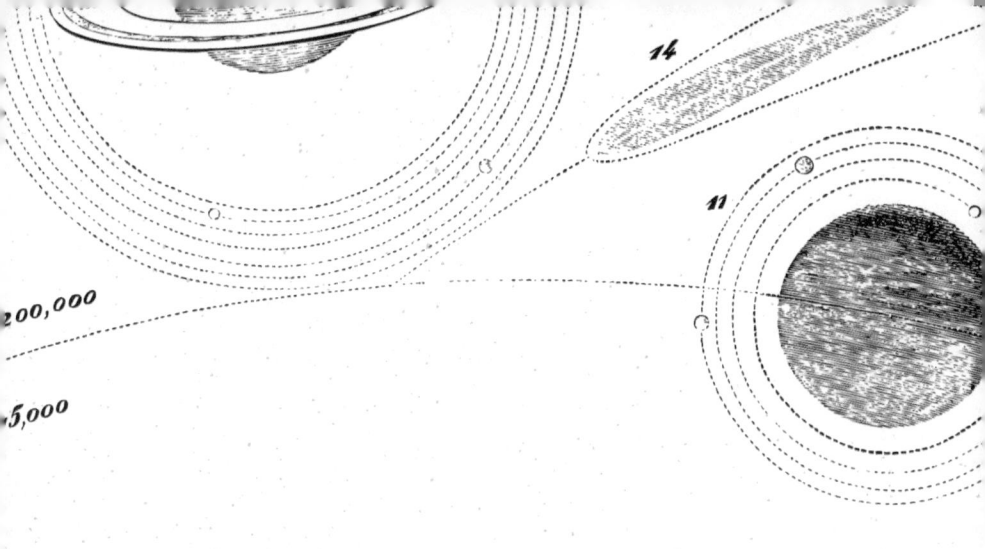

PART TWO,
the art of affliction

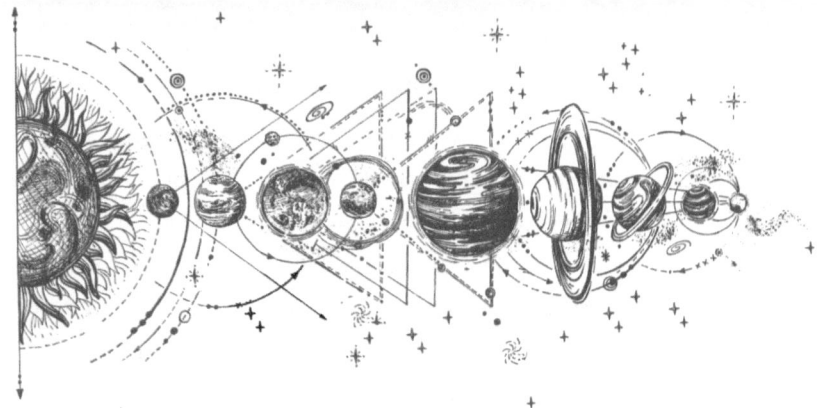

chapter thirteen.
bad days

Sometimes, the days are bad. And on those days, Nova finds herself trapped in her bedroom, the curtains drawn until nothing but darkness surrounds her, and her blanket covers her head. On the bad days, she finds herself thinking about her mother. On these days, when her hands are splayed against the counter in her bathroom, and the rain is pattering softly against the side of her apartment, she can see her mother's smile in her own. When she tilts her head to the side slightly, Nova sees her—*Marjorie.* She sees her beneath her watery pupils, so eerily dilated, and her cheekbones, which protrude in height. On the bad days, her lashes stick to her cheeks, dampness lines her under eyes, and sadness settles deep within her chest. On bad days, Nova sometimes wishes that sleep would overtake her for a little longer than normal—she wishes for a second that the world would cease.

There are moments throughout the day when Nova Magnolia Hawkins wishes for a second that she could forget her mother—and she finds that thought utterly suffocating. But sometimes, the pain is merely too hard to bear on the bad days. On these days, she hides. She hides because Nova is *happy*; Nova is *light*. Because sadness was not the

Hawkins way of living, according to her father, it was not meant to be within her nature to feel such heartening emotions. It was not tolerated.

She was allowed for only a week after her mother's death to cry—to mourn. Her father paid for a singular week of in-house therapy before he halted the visits altogether. Sadness was *weakness*, so instead, Nova smiled. She smiled, and she was light. She was happy.

She *hated* how much she looked like her mother, how much her smile and all the things that she thought made her uniquely herself belonged to Marjorie. Her deepened brown hair hanging in waves down her back, the freckles that pepper her nose, the beauty mark above her mouth. She shares her mother's eyes, the coffee-colored irises that shifted in the sun to a lightened caramel hue. She is her mother, and she figures, perhaps, that was why her father despises her so, why he fled instead of caring.

On the bad days, Indie is there. She would crawl into her bed in the middle of the night and pull her close. Indie would press a singular kiss to her nose and pull her head toward her chest. Indie would hum the lullaby that Nova's mother once whispered so sweetly in her ear and never move. She would hold Nova tight—and when Indie became too tired to stay awake, Sienna would sneak in and take her place. The blonde would hush Nova's cries and whisper sweet nothings until the brunette eventually cried herself to sleep.

Today is a bad day, perhaps the worst. And she finds herself in Chesterfield Park, nearing early morning. The sun hiding slightly behind the clouds, her knees are pressed roughly into her chest—and as she exhales, expelling the air trapped in her chest, Nova hears the faint crush of leaves.

A shadow casts upon her limbs, and the familiar scent only to be associated with Atlas Hale falling around her in flutters. She sniffs, turning her face away from his view before stating, "Indie sent you."

His shoulder brushes against her own as he lowers himself to the ground. His heat is suffocating. "Yes," was his response.

"M'fine." She lies so openly. So freely.

"Okay."

Silence follows.

"I haven't seen you in a few weeks," he says.

Because she was hiding. Because the realization was terrifying.

"I've been busy," she replies. "I'm sorry."

Silence echoes.

"I'm having a bad day," Nova tells him.

"Tell me what to do," Atlas frowns. "What do you need?"

She shrugs. Nothing works these days. She isn't sure.

"Can I..." His breaths are quick. "I'm going to try something. Just—don't move. Tell me if you want me to stop?"

She flinches as his heavy hand touches her shoulder. "What...?"

His free hand slips under her thighs, and she freezes at the contact. Nova hears her breath coming out in shudders and his own exhales fan her face. She glances up at him from beneath her lashes and sees the distraught, uncomfortable look on his face.

"Atlas." She presses a hand against his chest.

He ignores her, his movements continuing until she's on his lap. He breathes deeply from his nose, jaw clenching. Atlas hates to be touched, he hates it more than anything.

On bad days, Nova ponders why her mother did it. She wonders how she could refuse a trial that wished to save her life. Sometimes, on the bad days, Nova wonders how her mother could be so selfish.

Her shoulders brush his chest, and as his hands cradle the back of her head, Nova feels the familiar dampness flood her eyes. She fights back a closed chest sob and allows her head to fall to the crook of his neck. His breaths are irregular and shallow, but he never removes his hand. No, instead, he holds her tighter despite his discomfort.

"No more bad days alone," he says after a moment.

She lets out a sob-coated laugh. "No more bad days alone."

His pinky hooks with her own, which makes her laugh more.

"Promise me," he begs.

"*Promise.*"

On the bad days, Atlas is there. He answers her call and sits on her bed until morning. On the bad days, when Nova looks in the mirror and sees her mother, when she feels abandoned, Indie and Sienna are there. Rowan comes sometimes, too. On the bad days, when all Nova sees is her mother and who her father wants her to be—her friends remind her of who she is.

Sometimes, on the bad days, the hurt doesn't linger until night.

Sometimes, the bad days turn into good. And sometimes they don't. But Atlas is there, Indie is there, Sienna is there, and so is Rowan.

Sometimes, the days are bad, and that's okay.

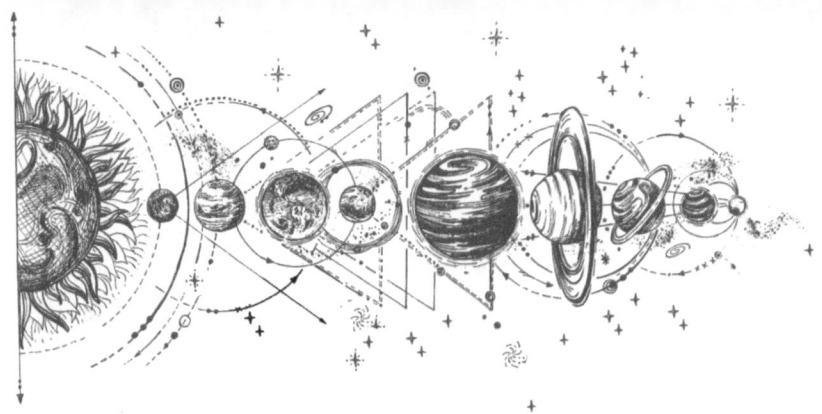

chapter fourteen.
ursa major

Sometimes, Nova Hawkins can feel impending sadness and heartache. She can practically taste the imminent doom—*salty* but sickeningly sweet in the same. She feels despair almost constantly. It will never leave her, almost as though it is a second skin.

It began at the ripe age of ten when her pet chinchilla had died. And as insignificant as the event was in the vast scale that was her life, it was the beginning of what Nova believed to be the *end* of her happiness. After that day, it seemed like everything had gone downhill perpetually fast, and she found herself living in communion with the pain. She became accustomed to the *arcane* and bitter taste that lingered on her tongue. Although she had felt a momentary reprieve when her father had come home with a pet cat—the peace lasted for only a few days before her life shattered to pieces at her small feet.

Nova remembers the day of her mother's cancer diagnosis like it was yesterday, as though it were tattooed on her brain, replaying on a

constant loop. She remembers the hushed tone of the doctor, how he spoke with sympathy and slight hopefulness. He attempted to whisper, but Nova knew. The doctor used big words and charts to discuss treatments, but she knew, even then—there was no hope. When they retreated to the car after, her mother told her that she was merely sick with a horrible cold. And that it would last for a long time.

But Nova wasn't stupid. She remembered Katie Harper's mother dying from cancer when they were eight. She remembered praying every night for her friend's family. She and her parents attended the funeral out of respect, but Nova never saw Katie again after that. The young girl's father had moved town, citing that Sailor Ridge held too many memories of Katie's mother and that staying wasn't healthy.

Nova remembered praying that night after the funeral to whoever could hear her that her mother would be safe from cancer.

Life was a sick joke. *Comical*, really.

Pain is a lonesome friend—her best friend. The kind of friend that never leaves your side for too long, always there.

She walked through life those days after with a slight smile, the one that never quite raised too high. The ones that were weighed down by a heaviness that surrounded the depths of her soul. Nova's mother had always said that the stars lived among her smile, so she put one on, wore it, and faked it—because her mother was sad enough without her baggage. She began to wear it so much that it felt *real* to smile.

Sometimes, she would see her mother smile because of it.

And Nova figured if she had to fake it for as long as she could, *she would*. She would pretend for Marjorie—she would smile for her.

Somewhere, amid her fake smiles, they became real.

Her mother eventually got better—the chemotherapy worked.

Her mother got better, and so Nova's smiles became real.

But life was funny in that way. Funny in that it gave you glimpses of happiness before snatching it away again. Before leaving you empty.

Her parents divorced when Nova was fourteen.

She didn't see her father much after that, only on holidays and a few random weekends. She lived with her mother in a cramped two-bedroom on the other side of town. But her mother was okay, so Nova was too. Everything was okay. She was happy for once. Free.

Nova went through life for years with just herself and her mother. The way that it had always been. Marjorie and Nova.

Life was *great*, even.

Life was *amazing*, even.

Life was good—until it wasn't.

Her mother's cancer came back when she was seventeen.

This time, it was worse.

So much worse.

Her mother decided against treatment.

This time, it was worse.

No matter how much Nova begged, Marjorie refused.

Life was good—until it wasn't. Not anymore.

Sometimes, Nova Hawkins can feel impending sadness and *heartache*. She can practically taste the imminent doom—*salty* but sickly sweet all in the same. She feels heartache almost constantly. Like it will never leave her, almost as though it is a second skin. She doesn't quite know why, but throughout the majority of her life, pain had been a constant friend. She found herself living in communion with the pain. She became accustomed to the *arcane* and bitter taste that lingered on her tongue. Pain was a friend for the lonely and brokenhearted. And Nova felt pain far more these days than anyone should. She carried it—lugged it along behind smiles and laughter.

Sometimes, Nova Hawkins can feel impending sadness and heartache. Sometimes, the pain is a bit too much—much like today.

Sometimes, the sadness is far more frequent than she ever wishes.

And *gosh*, it hurts. It hurts so badly, so suddenly at times, that she can hardly breathe. Her exhales become staggered, and the air she inhales fails to return to her body. God, sometimes it hurts—

"And when I went to leave this morning—he tried to ask me on a date," Sienna drones, "and that's never happened before, and I completely froze. Usually, guys are fine with casual sex. I don't know what to do. It's a shame, though—the sex was good, like mind-blowing. He just had to ruin it completely. What's the point of casual sex if you want to date?"

Nova blinks. Her ears are ringing, and her vision is blurry.

She finds herself responding on autopilot to her friend.

She can hardly even place the time.

Sometimes, she wants to give in. Wants to forget.

Sometimes, the pain is too much, and she wants to forget.

Is that truly so bad?

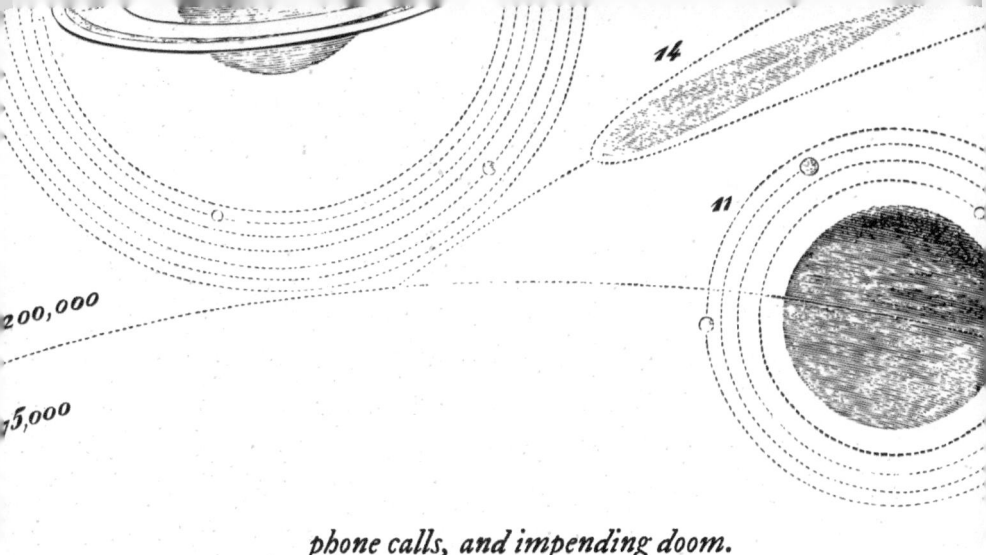

phone calls, and impending doom.

It's a Thursday when Atlas receives the call. It's quick at first, and the phone barely rings for over fifteen seconds. The number is unfamiliar but local, so he pays it no mind. The number is unknown, so he doesn't answer. He's walking toward the convenience store; his strides are lazy, and his fingers hold a cigarette. He knows Murray will throw a fit when he shows up, but the week has been stressful—the cigarette helps. The breeze is haunting. The darkness is creeping in far earlier, and Thanksgiving is drawing closer. The leaves are dying, and every semblance of October had seemingly drifted away—covered and replaced by deepened red decorations and the occasional sprouts of green around town. Atlas hates how fast time has passed. How rushed. He feels as though he can't keep up.

His phone rings again when his feet enter the quaint store, and the cool air dissipates. He fetches it out of his pocket, but this time, he forgets to check the caller ID. He hears breathing on the line.

"Hello?" he grumbles.

There's a brief intake of breath.

"Parker, I don't have time for your shit, dude."

There is silence.

"Goodbye, Parker."

"*Wait—Atlas? It's…oh, sweet boy. It's your mama.*"

It's barely enough words to fill a crossword puzzle. It would never win you another round in *Wheel of Fortune*, but it's enough to make him stumble. It's enough for his heart to plummet.

"*I…Atlas? Are you th—*"

His thumbs hit the end call button before she can finish.

Do you know that feeling when you're submerged under water, and it's becoming hard to breathe? Your limbs feel increasingly heavy, the weight of the ocean is waning on you, and for a moment, a split second, you think that you'll drown. You fight, and you fight until your arms are tired—your lids are faltering. And for a moment, you see spaces, flickers of your life. You think about everything and everyone.

That is how Atlas feels at this moment. Damien calls it impending doom. When you know death is coming and the end is near.

You can feel it.

You can nearly taste it.

At this moment, Atlas feels impending doom far more than anyone should ever be allowed to.

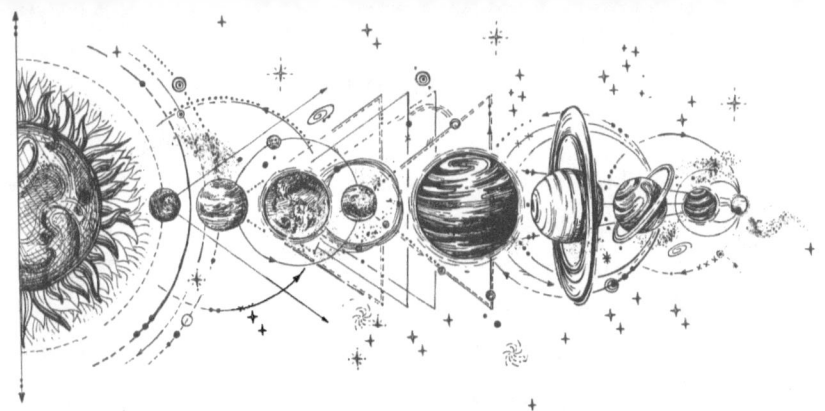

chapter fifteen.
haunting pasts, and nova hawkins

The night starts the same as always, with leftover Chinese takeout.

Atlas stands at the island, his elbows perched against the cool marble, while a headache the size of *Canada* pounds against his skull. The flickers of light from the pendants overhead cause the pressure to increase with every inhale he takes, but his mind is far too preoccupied to care about the pain. He eats like a man starving—cold noodles had never tasted so good—and a groan threatens to escape past his lips.

"You good?" Damien asks from the doorway, his shoulder resting against the frame. "Kind of late, isn't it?"

Atlas merely grunts in response.

"You got any more left?" Damien cranes his neck.

Atlas threatens to roll his eyes, but he places the half-eaten container to the left of him and beckons his friend over. "Eat." He hands Damien

a spare set of chopsticks. "You want sauce? Got that weird shit you like." Duck sauce. It was far too sweet and tangy for Atlas' immature taste buds, but Damien loves it, so he gets a handful weekly. "Here."

Damien claps his shoulder. "Thanks."

Silence settles again, and the sound of plastic colliding with paper fills the air. So much is said beneath the silence—in the darkness.

"You gonna tell me what's going on with you?"

"Nothin' worth talkin' about," Atlas grumbles.

His friend scoffs. "Try again." He digs into his food. "You're a shit liar—always have been. What's going on with you?"

Atlas has never been quite fond of memories. The kind that reverberates against your head, the kind that never leaves. Sometimes, he does well at controlling and pushing them aside, but as of late, they seem to continuously pound—knocking at the door near the forefront of his brain, threatening to break it down. And it's hard. The memories. They scatter about, looming almost too heavily like it's waiting for a downpour. And sometimes, he can't control when they come about. Or when the sadness is too much to bear, he can't handle it anymore.

"Feel stuck," he shrugs as though the words don't hold the weight of fifteen semi-trucks. "It just feels like it used to—like I'm walking through life weighed down by mistakes that don't even belong to me."

He remembers the day that his mother left him and his father like he only lived it moments ago. And sometimes he wonders if maybe he had gone straight home rather than stopping at Damien's if his mother would've seen his face and rethought her decision. He remembers how cold the house had been—how empty. Like a burial ground, except it was his death and not hers. Atlas doesn't remember anything about the months after she left, or at least he tries not to.

"Did she call again?" Damien has moved closer; their shoulders are touching. "I can talk to Mom. She can send her more money."

His mother started calling a few weeks ago. Atlas figures she got his number from his father, but she calls—she calls when she needs extra cash for drugs or food. She calls him '*sweet boy*,' and her voice sounds like molten honey. She sounds like she used to. But with a croak wasn't there before; something far more conniving lingers.

And he wishes that he hadn't fallen for it. The sickeningly sweet timbre and how she hugs him when he delivers her cash. The way she lies and says that she's trying and that she is sorry. But Atlas misses it; he misses being wanted. Misses her cherry and bergamot perfume. Misses her smile even if it is cracked. He misses his mother.

He misses his life.

When he sees Nova again, after the few weeks it's been, Atlas feels a weight lift from his shoulders. She wears an orange sweater with ribbons tied to the end of her sleeves. She's smiling, which differs from her previous tear-stained face and disheveled appearance, but—she's Nova.

"Hey." His shoulders brush against her own. She hands him a cup of coffee. "Thanks." The warmth defrosts his freezing hands.

The pair walk in silence, their steps falling into likened strides.

"You okay?" The question is so simply Atlas—so easy.

"Yeah." She nods with a slight smile. "Yeah, I'm okay."

At least one of them is, Atlas thinks.

"Are you okay?" Nova reiterates the question.

For a moment, Atlas thinks he might spare her his trauma. But there's something comforting in Nova; something about her makes even the worst things not as bad. So instead, he says, "No. No, I'm not."

November has come, so the air is much more frigid. Her cheeks are a scarlet red, and her eyes are watery from the harsh wind. He notes how cold her hands are when she takes his hand in her own. The touch is natural—slightly hesitant, but Atlas finds it feels nice. Like he's wanted, and that was all he had ever wanted. She interlaces their fingers, but she doesn't speak much. She doesn't even so much as look at him. She just holds his hand—and the words are clear, no matter how unspoken.

She squeezes once and again before letting go completely.

He wants to grab her hand again for a second, but that's not them. They're friends. The longer her touch lingers—the harder he knows it will be to let go when this is all over. The bucket list is twenty-five tasks that, once completed, will be the end of them.

This is temporary, as are most things in his life. For what reason would Nova be any different from the rest of them?

"It's my mom," he tells her. "She called a few weeks ago."

She recoils at the words. She doesn't know much. He hasn't told her, but she knows the basics. How unwanted he is. How his mother left. How he isn't enough, not even for his own mother to stay.

Atlas wonders if it's insensitive to talk about how much he hates that his mother is back when her own mother is dead. But her concerned gaze begs to differ. Atlas merely shakes his head. "It's fine," he lies.

"It's not," Nova assures him. "Have *you*...spoken to her?"

"Yeah." He figures telling her that Abigail calls once a week to ask for more money to buy drugs would falter the mood even more.

His clipped tone is enough to garner silence from Nova.

"Which task is it today, Hawkins?"

His quick change in conversation is whiplash-inducing.

"Uh," she fumbles over her words, "no tasks. I figured we could catch up. We haven't seen each other in a few weeks, so."

He hums a response. The walk to the park is short—quiet the rest of the way. He walks at her side, his eyes training on the gravel.

"Your shoes are untied," he notes.

"It's okay. Besides, when is it not?" Her smile is small at the memory from what seems like ages ago. He smirks—having the same thought.

"Gimme your foot." Atlas catches her arm.

The moment feels the same, except this time, they feel aged almost. Like so much time has passed but hasn't. It's been a month. Three since they'd known each other. Moments seemed to pass like road signs. Blurry, out of focus from how quickly the time was moving.

Nova shakes her head at his words, a laugh teetering on her tongue. "I can do that myself, you know?" Her heel digs into his thigh, and her hands steel themselves on his bicep. "But thanks."

"Just tryin' to be a gentleman, Hawkins."

Their proximity is close, and they're nearly the same height from his bent posture. Her hands clutch his bicep as his quickened movements jerk her forward. There's this odd electric current pulsing through the air. She can smell his cologne. Feel his warmth. His Adam's apple bobs as he glances at her from beneath hooded eyes. Hooded blue eyes that refuse to tell her any secrets—any thoughts. She watches him as he knots her shoe. She watches his concentration. How careful he is not to touch her more than needed. He's so oddly careful. So precise.

"You hugged me—the other week. I know you; I know that it's not something that you enjoy doing, but you calmed me down, anyway. Thank you. I'm sorry I wasn't there for you with your mom."

"S'fine." He moves on to her other shoe. "It's not like I even told you. It's fairly new. Besides, it's not your job to check in on me."

"We're friends, aren't we?"

The question holds so much more beneath the surface.

He searches her eyes, and his gaze is haunted. "Yeah." Her foot falls to the ground with a *thud*. "We're *friends*, Hawkins."

That's all that he has room for, anyway. All that he'll allow.

"Best friends?" She wiggles her brows.

He laughs—it is short. Forced. "Damien might have to kill you."

"He came by the other day. Well, to *Connies*. We talked a bit."

Of course, he did, Atlas thinks. *Asshole.*

"Oh yeah? What did he say?"

"Besides that, you were an asshole?" She snorts. "He said that you do this thing where you shut everyone out. He says that I shouldn't take it personally, though. That it's 'just you.' What you do when you're scared someone might be getting too close."

Well damn, Atlas thinks.

"What'd I tell you about trying to be my therapist, Hawkins?"

"Friendships don't work unless we talk," Nova pointed out.

"Is that what this is? I don't *need* a therapist," Atlas snaps.

Nova stops short at his tone. "What is happening? Why are you so upset with me right now? We're friends. And something is hurting you; anyone with eyes can see that. I want to help—you can talk to me."

Atlas scoffs, his eyes rolling at her words. "God, I don't need help Nova. You see the world through rose-colored lenses. Like a child has scribbled across it to the point of no return. You're blinded. You can't see outside of your—very odd might I add—notion of the world around you. Your head," he sneers, taps softly against her temple, "is filled with knights in shining armor. But that isn't the world, Nova. The world is dark, and it is unforgiving sometimes. No one is here to save us. That is our reality. You can't fix me." He taps his chest. "If I'm not broken. You need to wake up, Hawkins. Smell the *fucking* roses. Shit happens, life is shitty, and I'm completely okay with it. You can't fix me. When we met, do you think I didn't see how you looked at me? I'm a project for you."

"That is not true." She shakes her head.

"Yes, it is."

"No," Nova defends. "You agreed to the list. You wanted a chance to feel something. You might see the world as this disgusting place, but I don't. Life sucks—we aren't children. But I refuse to think like you. Do you honestly think that I don't understand the reality of life? That I'm so naive that I can't see suffering? My mother is dead. My father doesn't even speak to me anymore. You're not the only victim here, Atlas. But I refuse to let those things run and ruin my life."

Her voice is so skewed, so pain-filled that he can barely stand it.

"I'm not doing this right now," Atlas dismisses her.

"Where are you going?" She pulls at his arm. "What is happening right now? Why are you so upset with me, Atlas?"

He turns to face her, and for once, Nova can see his defeat. How exhausted he is. His face is crumbled, and his eyes are tired.

"It's not you. I'm not mad at you." He rubs a thumb over his brow. "I've got a lot of stuff going on. I'll see you around, Nova."

"Atlas," she calls after him.

But his steps are retreating and retreating until he's a blur.

He shows up at her apartment later that evening, around two o'clock in the morning. Her feet echo against the cool wood as she rushes toward the front door, hoping not to wake her roommates. When Nova opens the door, a look of question falls on her tired face. Atlas stands before her with a hoodie on, his breath catching weight in the wind. His eyes are red and tired, and his hands are shoved into his coat pockets, balled into fists.

His posture is odd, waning. Defeated almost.

"Atlas?" she says, taking him in.

"Did you get my calls?" he asks in a rushed tone. "I tried calling you a few times. But it kept going to voicemail," Atlas reiterates.

Her attire consists of an oversized t-shirt and sleep shorts. Her feet are bare. "Atlas," Nova says his name again, her brow pinching, "it's nearly"—Nova checks her phone—"two in the morning." She frowns. "Are you okay?" Concern riddles her voice. She is worried.

"What?" He glances at her outstretched phone. "Oh. I didn't—I think I lost track of time at some point. I hadn't realized it was so late."

"Are you okay?"

"I shouldn't have spoken to you the way that I did earlier," he simply rushes out. "The thing with my mom is getting to me, and instead of talking about it, I lashed out. It's hard because people don't usually care if I'm okay. I'm not used to people caring so much. So, I'm sorry."

He rummages in his pocket before pulling a piece of paper out. "I wrote this. It's a list. Of the things that you might want to know. As a friend, of course, about me. Likes and dislikes. Fears and stuff."

"Of course." She takes the paper carefully in her hand. She holds it like it's a prized possession—sacred to her. "Yes. I mean. Thank you."

He merely nods curtly.

There's hope in her eyes.

He clears his throat, nodding again before retreating down the steps. He makes it about halfway—nearly to his car when he feels something crash into his back. It takes him a moment to register what happened. But her arms are wound around his waist, her face buried in his dampened hoodie—and her breathing is erratic.

He freezes for a moment and starts to open his mouth.

"Shut up." She silences him. "Just hug me back and shut up."

His hand slowly reaches up to cradle the back of her neck. He's shaking slightly, but he holds her so gently like she'll break or worse, disappear. His free arm loops around her waist, pulling her up slightly until she's flush against his chest. Until her warmth halts his cold.

The hug is so Nova. So distinctly Nova that it hurts. He feels almost unworthy to experience something so intimate with her.

"I'll write one too," she says into his chest. "It'll be our secret. A list of our stars—our flaws and our dreams. Just for us."

He can't speak. He can't move.

"Thank you for trusting me," she whispers.

Atlas wonders if trust has always been this easy. So simple.

Is it truly made up of just these things?

Or is it simply Nova? Is that what had been missing?

The air was frigid, biting and nipping at their exposed skin, but the pair didn't care much. It is just them—the moon, the stars.

Just Nova and Atlas.

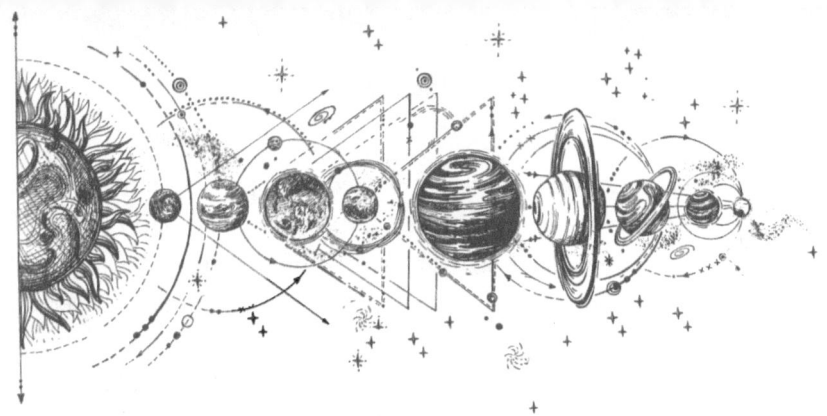

chapter sixteen.
mother knows best

two weeks ago

Atlas feels a substantial amount of dread. He feels dread far more at this moment than any person should. At this moment, as his back presses against the cool bench, Atlas feels an ache in his chest that he cannot shake. He notes that her hair is still the same shade of brown, mousey but *dull*—like it's dried or lifeless. Her eyes are the same shade of blue as his own, but there's a tinge around her irises that wasn't there before. He also notes that her pupils are enlarged. Her chapped lips are flaked with blood and there's dirt beneath her fingernails. A pungent scent of something arcane, salty, and stale fills his nostrils.

"Thank you…thanks for meeting me *he*-here."

She's skin and bones, Atlas notices.

And her words are coming out slurred, choppy, and unorganized.

He can't speak; he can't move. There is an ache building in his stomach, and it sits there against his ribcage, making it insufferably hard to breathe. So, instead, he nods once and again before averting his eyes.

"You've gotten so big." Her hands are cold, and the sudden touch causes him to flinch. Abigail's mouth screws up, and a look he can't quite decipher wanes on her face. "You look *lik*...like your father. You've grown so much. Have you been eatin' okay? I remember how hard it was to get you to eat when you were younger." She chuckles, "You hated peas. I remember having to mush them up with your peaches to ge—"

"What are you doing here, Abigail?" Atlas cuts her off mid-sentence. "Surely it isn't to revisit happy memories. So what are you doin' back here? If you're looking for Dad, he's long gone."

She tugs at her sleeves; the movements are erratic, quick, and jumpy. Her hands are shaking, and Atlas notes she hasn't sat still since she arrived only moments ago. "I *mi*...missed you." She croaks. She *lies*.

"Try again," he presses. "That's a lie. We both know it. What are you doing back here? Come to check in on the things you've left behind, is that it? Well, I'm fine." Atlas sniffs, clicking his tongue. "Perfect."

"I know I'm *n*—not your favorite person." She twitches. "That I've made some..." She mouths her words oddly, and her tongue runs along her lip as she fights to uphold the conversation. "Really b...bad mistakes." Abigail withdrew a breath. "But I wanna change. I want to be better."

The lies seem to run from her mouth like warmed honey. She's sweating like a sinner in the front pew of a church, or perhaps it's because this is the longest she's gone without being coked up. Atlas is unsure, but he knows that she's full of shit. He remembers his father once telling him that his mother is a pathological liar, that she lies for sport. That her nature knows nothing else. It isn't until today that he realizes his father was right. From a young age, in his eyes, his mother could do no wrong. Atlas attempted to protect the image of her in his head for years. He thought that if he could preserve the person she was before everything changed—he would be able to forgive her.

But as she sits at his side, shaking, stumbling over her words, and tugging mindlessly at her hair—Atlas realizes he never wants to see her again. His fabricated memories of her are enough for him.

"How much will get you to go away and never come back?"

Abigail jerks. "I—well, I lost my job a few days ago." She tugs harshly at her battered shirt. "And..." She purses her lips and smacks. "I will need some money t—to get back." She bites down on her lips as though she's contemplating. "I think that—a thousand would do fine."

"*A thousand*," he repeats. He mouths the word and feels it around before a chuckle escapes him. "You want a thousand dollars?"

"After everything I have done for you—I deserve somethin' some type of *compens...sation*. You know, you nearly killed me when I gave birth to you. That medical bill put your daddy and me in a lot of debt."

He sits for a moment. His eyes are trained ahead on the nearest tree, and they burn—tears are pricking in the edges, and his jaw clenches so tight he's afraid he might break his teeth. He thinks back to all the times when he watched his friends run into their mother's arms. He thinks back to the moments when he wished and prayed for the day she would walk back into his life. It's comical. He thinks back to every moment when his mother should've been there, and instead, he sees Catie Hawthorne in her place, whispering sweet nothings in his ears.

At every Little League game, every award for his art. When he broke his arm, jumping off the swing. He remembers the first time he had his own room at the Hawthorne's, only a few doors down from Damien. Atlas thinks about when he got accepted into college and how the Hawthornes paid his tuition. How Catie called him *son*. How the Hawthorne's bought him his first car. He has a mother. Catie Hawthorne is his mother. No matter how much he looks like the woman sitting next to him—Abigail Turner is not his mother. She is nothing more than a body, a random woman who is in his memories in glimpses.

"I hate you," Atlas says, and he means it. "So much."

He has spent his entire life wondering how this moment would play out. And he never imagined that those would be the words he said.

"You left me," he continues, "when I needed you. You didn't *raise* me. You gave birth to me, but that was all you've ever done. You have never been my mother. Catie Hawthorne is my mother."

"That bitch is not your mother," Abigail sneers. "She's only ever wanted to make me look bad. I t...tried Atlas. I wanted to be there for you. I wanted to be better. But, I'm...messed up. She is not the savior you think that she is. She's some rich—no good *bitch*. She turned you against me. I know she did. She's no good for you, Atlas," she pants.

Atlas holds his hand up, silencing her. "Here." He holds out an envelope. "There's more than what you asked for in there. I don't care what you do with it—I don't care where you go. But you need to leave." He rises from his seat. "Take your money and get the hell away."

"*Atlas—*"

"Goodbye, Abigail."

He doesn't stick around to hear her excuses after that. He just walks. He's not quite sure where he's going, but he walks, and he keeps walking until he sees the familiar white picket fence and the dented mailbox that he hit his forehead on at the age of ten. He sees the familiar white home—the cobblestone driveway, the wrap-around porch that he's spent far too many times running around. He sees the chicken coop on the side of the house. Maisie is out and about, pecking the ground. Atlas doesn't stop walking until he hears the familiar rattle of the door against the frame. Until he smells cinnamon and thyme and hears the faint chatter from the television. He crosses the living room because he knows his mom. He knows she's gardening the same as always, tonight.

As he walks, he spots the old tire swing. The rope is dying, but it's still holding on by a thread. Catie is crouched down by her primroses.

And as he approaches her, Atlas can hardly keep it in. Even at his older age, despite the amount of life he's lived, there's something so comforting about the apron she wears around her waist and the bun that is always secured at the back of her head. Catie Hawthorne is home.

"You should know by now that I have eyes in the back of my head, Atlas. You should always know better than to try to sneak up on me when I'm holding my gardening tools," Catie chastises him.

He can't hold back his watery laugh. "Sorry, Mama."

It's his sniffle that causes her to turn. "Atlas? *Hey.*" Her voice is soothing. She stands, hardly brushing the dirt from her hands to cup his face. "Hey, sweet boy—what's going on?" She drops a free hand to rub his shoulder. "You're okay. *You're okay*, I'm right here."

Because no matter how old her boys got, Catie Hawthorne would never stop being their mother. Damien and Atlas were her boys, always.

He clings to her despite the height difference.

"*What's happened?*" He can hear Catie faintly ask.

He's crying too loud, too hysterically. He's nearly embarrassed by it, but this is his family. He's safe here. Always has been.

"*Abigail.*" Damien's voice fills his ear.

The string of curses that leave Catie's mouth is enough to make an angel cry. She pulls him closer. "Go get some warm milk."

"We're twenty-three. You know that, right?" Damien snorts.

"Shut up for once in your life and go get some milk."

Atlas hears a faint *thwack* followed by an *ouch*.

"It's okay," Catie promises.

But Atlas knows it isn't. Nothing about this feels okay.

Atlas Hale feels a substantial amount of dread. In this moment, he feels dread far more than any person ever should.

chapter seventeen.
beneath the moon

present day

Something that Atlas has long since noticed about Nova is that she tends to ask the oddest questions. So randomly, so without thought, that at times it approaches him with the strength of the wind. They're on the back of his truck again—merely gazing up at the stars when she asks her first question of the evening. The genuine contemplation of her voice and the mixture of slight pain is enough to make him glance down at her.

"Atlas," she begins. "Do you think this is all worth it—the pain? Do you think that everything we've gone through in life will be worth it in the end, when all this is said and done? Do you think it's worth it?"

No, he threatens to say. But this is Nova; he can't hurt her that way. So instead, he says, "This life is filled with pain. It is riddled with

nothing but suffering, but despite it, we have good things. We have our friends and family that care about us." He hesitates before speaking again, "Besides, anything that put you in my life can't be that bad, can it?"

She turns on her side, the cool metal from the truck bed pinching at her exposed forearms as she glances up at him. "You like me." A Cheshire smile slowly appears on her face. "You *actually* like me, Atlas Hale. And here I thought you despised the mere thought of me."

He shakes his head, scowling, but there's slight amusement lingering in his eyes. "Yeah—you're not horrible." His fingers trail down her arm absentmindedly. "Perhaps a bit annoying at times, but I've grown quite fond of your company these past few months, Nova Hawkins."

Sometimes, Atlas sees her, and he feels as though his soul is singing to the clouds. Like his soul is singing praises in her midst. In her presence, Atlas seems to find himself so consumed with a startling amount of peace that he questions whether she was a sorcerer. For a moment, a brief second within her presence, Atlas feels as though perhaps God is real to some capacity. Perhaps they are kind. To be in Nova's midst, the heavens, the earth, and all things particularly odd within the world, seem to be perfect—glorious even. If Nova Hawkins exists, so must all things that breathe life and share love.

Perhaps life is okay.

There's a brief silence, and a humming from the breeze is all that can be heard. Her hair is fanned out around her, and her head brushes his chest; his chest rises and falls with the falling of the November leaves. His breathing has evened out, and every exhale fuels the soft flutters of touches he begins to leave down her arm. Silence seems to follow them wherever they go, but it's the good kind. The soft, gentle kind of silence that pulses through the air with delicate touches.

"You are not as dark as you wish to seem, Atlas Hale," Nova says randomly. "Not by a long shot. You're just a bit broken. But we all are."

"Why is it that every deep conversation we've ever had is outside?" Atlas attempts to change the subject. There's something in her stare that he can't quite decipher, and he decides that he'd rather not.

Nova teases, "Maybe we're part werewolf."

"Nah, I can't see it." He shakes his head. "You're too soft to be a werewolf. You're more like—well, you remind me of a baby deer."

Nova purses her lips. "A deer," she repeats. "You think out of all the animals on earth, I would be a freaking deer?"

"You say it like it's a bad thing."

"Do you know how many deer get killed on the highways daily because they're too stupid to notice a moving car? And you think I'm a deer, of all things?"

"Is this one of those questions that I should answer carefully?"

"Yes. This shapes the integrity of our *re*-friendship." Nova catches her slip-up. She pauses to check his reaction, but he gives none. So she figured he hadn't heard her at all. "This is life or death."

"You are a wren bird," he answers with ease. "Small, but you're big—you are known in all the ways that count, Nova. You love purely, loudly. You've suffered through loss and pain, but yet, still smile."

"Oh." She's at a loss for words. Nova doesn't quite know what to say to him or if she should even speak at all. So instead, she simply says, "Thank you." Because it is all that she can muster the courage to speak.

"It's the truth." Atlas shrugs, grunting as he pushes himself up. "No need to thank me for the truth." He stretches his arms.

"You wouldn't be an animal." Nova tells him, "You would be a star. The brightest star in the sky. You wouldn't be able to go unnoticed."

Atlas could never be invisible; he had the kind of presence that stuck with you—that never went away or wavered. Perhaps that was the reason she hadn't forgotten him after that day in the park. And why she had been so eager to see him again. He was an enigma, and as much as Nova knew that she shouldn't, she cared far more about him than she had ever meant to. It was obvious, the attraction, from the day she met him. He was gorgeous—but it had been nothing more than that, not in the beginning, at least. But the more she knew him, the more she saw him laugh and smile; the more she knew who Atlas truly was, the harder she fell. And perhaps it was simply infatuation that piqued interest because of the list. Whatever it was, Nova knew it was no longer friendship.

"I don't feel like a star. I feel like a bloated whale." Atlas snorts. "Deep in the ocean, drowning, and only coming up to breathe."

Nova sits up at his words, her brow furrowed in concern. Atlas merely shakes his head and brushes her off. "Sorry," he murmurs lowly. "I didn't mean to dampen the mood. What were you saying?"

"Nothing that important." She waves him off. "How are you doing anyway, after everything with *you*...Abigail."

They talked a bit a few days ago, not that Atlas gave much anyway, besides the fact that his real mother was named Abigail.

"S'fine," Atlas deflects. "Besides, this isn't about me. This is about the list—why else are we on the back of my truck at a crusty gas station?" He gestures to the empty lot. "What are we even doing?"

"If I'm being honest." Nova stifles a laugh. "I just wanted a slushie." She breaks into a fit of giggles at the look on his face. "I'm sorry, okay? You wouldn't go with me otherwise. Hey!" She slaps his hand away from her hair. "Do not—it took me hours," Nova warns.

"Oh yeah? It took me an hour to drive here." He pokes her side playfully. "What the hell, Hawkins?" Atlas reaches for her again.

"Stop—ah!" Nova squeals as his hands graze her side.

"Are *you*...ticklish?" His smirk is mischievous.

"No," she heaves, taking in the look on his face. "No. Stop." Nova stands slowly. "Don't you dare—I swear, Atlas. No!"

Her squeals fill the air around them. His laughter mixes in alongside it, and the sound is so foreign that he has to pause for a moment. He watches as she clambers from the truck bed, still giggling as she fights to get away from him. His movements are faster because he catches her waist before she can even make it a mere two feet away. Nova gasps a laugh, thrashing in his arms as his fingers dance along her sides, traveling up her back. He's laughing—full-on belly laughing. Her cheeks are red, and her smile is blinding—radiant. And even with her hair falling and flying in the wind, Atlas notes that she still looks beautiful. Nearly iridescent. She's so perfect, so Nova.

"Give in," he mumbles against the back of her neck.

"Never," she breathes, giggling, as he spins her around.

"Give in, Hawkins." She's facing him now.

Out of breath, Nova grips his jacket lapels. She realizes that he is holding her so flush against his chest that she feels his heart beating. His chest moves up and down erratically, coinciding with her own, and his face is mere inches from hers—his nose grazes her hairline, and she can feel the warmth of his breath fanning across her face. There's a singular strand of hair, laying so perfectly on his forehead that she can't help but reach out to brush it away. Atlas tightens his grip at her movements, his eyes training back on hers. Blue and brown collide.

"Give in," he whispers, though this time Nova is unsure of what he means. His left hand reaches up slowly, his fingers threading through the hair at her neck, the slight pressure causing her chin to tip up.

Atlas lets out what seems to be a struggled groan. He's surrounded by her, consumed by her. Everywhere he looks is Nova. He sees her in the trees and can hear her laugh in the evening breeze; she's branded in the forefront of his mind. He thinks about her almost constantly, more than any normal person should—she's addicting.

"*Atlas...*" she utters his name as though it's a prayer. Like she'll do anything, be anything for him. And it tears him up on the inside.

"Wrenning Bird," he murmurs against her temple.

"What?" she whispers, her eyes training on his lips.

"Wrenning Bird—you're a wren bird. *My* wren bird. Small, but you, Nova Hawkins, have a heart that is utterly loud and consuming."

"You're so..." She shakes her head at his words, tipping her chin further back to get a better look at him. For some reason, her eyes are stinging. "I don't think I've ever met anyone quite like you, Atlas."

"Good." His lips flutter along her hairline. "Because neither have I. You are truly one of a kind, little Wrenning Bird."

Everything about this moment is so *them*. So perfectly Nova and Atlas. Random from the moment they met, a bit awkward and scattered, but it's them. They are Atlas and Nova—a bit misunderstood, but they are Atlas and Nova. And that is completely okay.

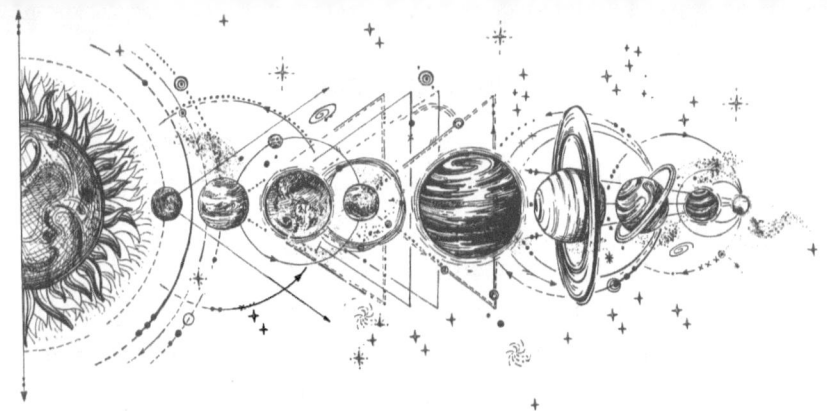

chapter eighteen.
movie nights, and wrenning birds

She likes it when he smiles, Nova notices. She likes the *fullness* of his lips and the crinkles that appear by his eyes—his eyes that glimmer, like the ocean filled with watercolors and clematis. How his cheeks rise, and how the faint flush of red settles among them from the cold. She likes it when he's concentrating, and his tongue peeks out from his lips, and his brow furrows. Nova figures she likes everything about Atlas Hale.

It is different; so much has changed after that day in the lot. The pair seems to touch one another more—faint flutters of desperate touches, soft trails of fingertips over limbs. Like now, as they sat amid their friends in the quaint booth in the back of *Connie's*, the tips of her fingers trail absentmindedly along his heart lines. Her eyes are trained on the menu, but her mind was elsewhere. His arm slung along the back of the booth, his own fingertips dancing along in ghost-like

touches on her shoulder. Like whispers, like fated secrets shared only between them.

"So, movie night—what are we watching?" Sienna asks.

"I vote Terminator," Parker offers, though he is met with silence. "Rude," he deadpans, "All right, assholes, what do you want to watch? And I swear if one of you says a chick flick, I'm leaving."

"Sexist much?" Sienna scoffs. "I vote Marvel."

"Boring much?" Parker shoots back. "Too many movies."

"Just say you're stupid and don't understand greatness when you see it, Parker, because the *Marvel Cinematic Universe* is God tier," Sienna defends, crossing her arms. "Robert Downey Jr. is elite. He needs to be protected at all costs and put into a museum to preserve his greatness."

"You do know that he doesn't know you, right?" Damien chimes in. "Like, at all. He doesn't know you exist."

"Oh, I'm sorry. Does anyone else hear an annoying voice?" Sienna cups her ear. "No, just me? Huh, how completely odd."

"You know, every day you give me another reason to dislike you, O'Connell," Damien snarks. "Seriously, why did I start hanging out with you? Besides the fact that you've got a nice"—Sienna raises her brow—"*smile*. You're potentially the most annoying person I've ever met."

"Gosh, it kills you how much you want me, doesn't it?" Sienna pats his arm sympathetically. "Admission is the first step to recovery."

"Don't touch me." Damien pushes her hand away as though it were some infectious disease. "I wouldn't touch you with a ten-foot pole, O'Connell. We both know that. Go flirt with someone else."

It was no surprise that Sienna is attracted to Damien. Anyone with eyes would be. He had brunet almost black hair—dark green eyes, and a smile that is nearly sinful. He's every girl's wet dream come to life. Although Nova garners that his nasty attitude might be the reason he doesn't have a girlfriend. They have spoken only a few times since that night at the Hawthorne's, and each time, she recounts, feels a bit more threatening than the last. He is always treading the line of outwardly telling her to stay away from Atlas, all while under the guise of protecting him. She isn't entirely sure if Damien likes her much.

He is a bit hard to read.

"Sorry, I'm late—work." Indie heaves as she adjusts her bag. "Did I miss anything important? Have you guys ordered yet?"

In the past two times over the course of the last week that Atlas and Nova's friends had begun to hang out, Nova noted that Indie seemed to be the only one outside of Atlas and Parker that Damien spoke to. But then again, Indie is Indie. What was not to love?

"No," Damien answers her as he moves slightly to the side. "We decided to wait for you. Well, *some* of us did," he says, eyeing Sienna.

"What? I was hungry, sue me. At least it was just an appetizer."

Rolling her eyes, Indie slides into the booth. "Thanks."

"Where's Micah, by the way?" Parker asks.

"Uh, Delly had ballet or something," Atlas chimes in.

"She's like three—can kids even walk that young?" Parker tilts his head. "Is she just going to crawl to the beat of Beethoven?"

"She's three—not a newborn, idiot," Damien grumbles.

"Is there supposed to be a difference…" Parker frowns.

Damien holds his finger to his mouth. "Just stop talking, please."

Nova shakes her head. It's moments like these that she cherishes the most. The laughter, the slight sense of camaraderie. Even though she hasn't known them long, Atlas' friends are slowly becoming her own. Which is far more than she garnered. It began with a simple bucket list that has led to nights beneath the stars, trips, friendships, and Atlas Hale. The night is perfect. So perfect.

"Dude, Team Cap, any day—are you *insane*?" The movie has been paused halfway through, and this argument has been going on ever since. "Hawkeye, Winter Soldier, Wanda Maximoff, and you honestly think that Team Iron Man ever had a fighting chance?"

"Yes?" Damien says in a *duh* tone. "He has the tech to knock them down at any given point. Yeah, Captain America had more players on his team with superpowers but Iron Man would've won."

Shaking her head, Nova rises from the couch. "I'm getting more popcorn. Does anyone want anything while I'm up?"

There is a round *"nopes"* that follows.

Laughing softly to herself, Nova wanders aimlessly into the kitchen, humming as she makes her way around the island. The once seasonal autumn decor in her apartment has long since been replaced with Christmas decor, thanks to Sienna, of course. Where Nova loved the autumn season, Sienna is obsessed with Christmas. She says that it reminded her of the East Coast, where her winters consisted of snow on the beach and trips to New York over the course of winter. Nova has always wondered how boring the holidays are here in comparison to the Coast. The Olympic Peninsula is nowhere near as beautiful.

Amid her thoughts, she feels the familiar warmth she has slowly become accustomed to sneaking up behind her. She can't stop the slight smile that appeared on her face. "You're getting pretty good at this," she notes as the man leans his chin against her shoulder.

"Oh yeah?" She can feel his smile, even if it was slight.

"Mhm. I'm proud of you," Nova admits as she turns.

"Had a good teacher," Atlas shrugs nonchalantly.

Atlas has slowly, if only slightly, began to accept hugs, which is far more than she expected from him. She isn't entirely sure where his touch aversion comes from, but it isn't her place to hound him about it. She knows bits and pieces of his life that he is willing to share, and that is enough for Nova for the time being. He is comfortable, and that is what matters the most to her, always.

Blushing, Nova decides to change the subject. "Did you need something?" she asks, moving to the side so that he could stand.

"Nah, the argument was uh—getting on my nerves."

"Ah, yes." Nova smiles. "So, which are you? Team Iron Man or Team Captain America?" she clarified, noting his furrowed brows.

"How about neither? Not a huge Marvel fan. My dad was, once. He uh…" Atlas cracks a small smile. "Used to make me watch them with him every Sunday whenever it came on FX—he's a huge comic nerd."

She notes a sense of sadness that creeps in at the mention of his father and glances away slowly, clearing her throat. "You should, um, I mean, do you talk to him much anymore?" Nova asks.

Atlas' face falters. "No. No, not really. I don't plan to."

"Yeah." She nods. "No, I get it. I just miss my dad sometimes. I wish that he would reach out and talk to me, you know? I just think that sometimes we take for granted the people that we still have. He's all I have left but, we hardly ever see each other. Last time we spoke, I heard he was getting married to some doctor—Sarah McCullen." She says her name with so much venom that it causes Atlas to flinch. "But he never really called much after that except to ask about Rowan."

"Ah yes, Rowan." His tone is sarcastic. "How is *Robert* doing?"

"I don't understand why you don't like him." Nova shakes her head as she moves around him to close the microwave. "You've met all of what, one time, and hardly even spoke. He's really sweet."

So is candy, Atlas thinks, *and yet it still gives you decaying teeth.*

"Don't know him well enough." Atlas shrugs. "He seems entitled. Like some pretty little rich boy who can cough wrong and have ten maids ready to wipe the very ground, he walks on. I hate people like that."

"Don't know him well enough, but you can make such large assumptions about him?" Nova raises her brow. "He's my friend."

"You like him or something?" Atlas asks from his lowered position against the counter. His bicep flexes as he shifts his weight.

Nova furrows her brow at his tone. "Would it bother you?"

"No," he responds quickly. "Your life, Hawkins. Figured you would keep better company than that. Sorry for trying to look out."

"He's my *friend*," she emphasizes. "Has been for a long time. He's a good guy, but we're just friends. Nothing more, nothing less."

"Even if he wants more?" Atlas questions.

Nova purses her lips, taking in his neutral expression. "You're making that face again," she points out to him. "You'll get wrinkles."

"Nova." Atlas pushed himself up. "You didn't answer me."

"Does it matter?" She sighs, standing on her toes to reach for the bowl in the top cabinet. "Life is weird—who knows what will happen."

He snags the bowl, handing it to her with a pointed expression. "Even if he wants more?" Atlas asks again, pushing the glass into her hands. "It's a simple question, Hawkins; just answer it."

"Why do you care so much, anyway?"

"I don't," he says. "I was just wondering."

Nova takes the bowl from his hand, searching his eyes briefly before saying, "Even if he wants more. I don't plan on dating Rowan."

There's something so entirely different hidden beneath those words. She knows it, and so does he. But neither of them said it.

"Good." He nods once and again. "Good girl, you're too young for a boyfriend anyway," Atlas jokes. "We have to protect your purity."

Nova snorts, moving around him. "That ship sailed a long time ago, buddy. Dustin Harper freshman year of college." She smirks at his shocked face. "You sure you don't want any popcorn? It's *delicious*."

Atlas frowns, "I hate you—so much."

Her laugh is all that's left behind as she leaves.

The night ends the same as it began, with Nova and Atlas. They're in her room—and he lounges lazily on her bed while she rummages through her clothes for one of her father's old t-shirts.

"Here." She tosses it to him. "It should fit."

"Thanks." He grunts as he sits up. "Are you sure it's okay that we all crash here? Your place isn't that big. We'll take up half the floor."

"Sure, besides. Tonight was fun. Unless you count the five arguments in the span of two hours, of course." She snorts.

He smirks. "Of course."

There's a brief moment of silence.

"I should change." Atlas gestures to the shirt. "Where's your bathroom?"

"Down the hall, third door on the left." She tells him, leaning back against her desk. "There's a spare toothbrush in the drawer closest to the shower. And you can use my body wash. I don't mind."

The second that he leaves the room, Nova sends herself into a frenzy. She all but rips her hair out as she combs through her tangled tendrils in an attempt to keep them at bay. Thankfully, she curled her hair earlier in the day, so it now falls in slight waves down her back. She moves on to slip off her dirtied sweats, pulling on a pair of cleaner, far nicer silk pajama shorts. Her T-shirt will have to do—it's the only clean one that she has, unfortunately. She should've done laundry. She sniffs her shirt and winces. It smells like the buttered popcorn she dropped on it hours ago.

"Is there anywhere I can put my clothes?"

Nova jumps at the sound of his voice. "Um." She smooths out her shirt. "You can give them to me. I'll throw them in the wash in the morning and give it back to you whenever I see you again."

"Cool." He nods. "I should head to the living room."

"You don't have to," she blurts the words before she can stop them, "I mean—you can, we can um. I—we can talk if you want."

"Talk," he repeats slowly. "You want to talk."

"Yep." She nods because that's exactly what she had so stupidly said. "We can talk." She takes in his face. "*Or not.* We don't have to."

His eyes drift down her body until they stop at her pajama shorts. He clears his throat. "Sure. We can talk."

"That's our thing," she adds before cringing. "I mean. We talk about a lot of things. Mostly very deep and emotional things."

"You're nervous," Atlas realizes.

"Yes, very."

"Why?" He furrows his brow. "It's me. It's *just* me."

"You're in my room," Nova states, taking a small step back when he comes closer. "What...are you doing?"

"I'm sitting?" He casts her an odd glance.

"On my bed?"

He raises a brow. "Would you rather I sit on the floor, Hawkins?"

"Yes. I mean no, I don't know. I'm nervous."

"C'mere." He beckons her closer. "Come on. We're way past this. Come here." He snags her arm. "Little closer—God, Nova. I'm not going to *fucking* kill you or something. For someone who invades my personal space every second of the day, you're being very odd about this."

"You've never been in my room like this before."

His legs are parted slightly as he pulls her to stand between them. Even in his seated position, she only comes to his nose. When she stiffens, Atlas rolls his eyes and yanks her closer. His sudden bout of movements jerk her forward until she's nearly flush against his chest. Atlas hums softly and wraps his arms around her waist, pulling her into a hug.

"See," he murmurs into her hair, "this isn't bad at all."

Huffing, Nova adjusts her chin against his shoulder, "Whatever."

"Lighten up, Hawkins. I don't bite."

Yeah, well, that's the problem, she thinks.

He stills, and for a moment, she wants to ask him what's wrong until she realizes her thoughts weren't solely in her head and that she's said them aloud. She said those words out loud, and he heard them.

"Oh God," she gasps. "I didn't mean that. Oh my gosh."

His laugh is so sudden that she flinches. He laughs, the kind of laugh that starts deep in your chest until it echoes throughout the room. And gosh, his laugh is beautiful. It's so beautiful that it hurts.

"Well," he says once he's sobered. "That's one way to kill tension. Geez, Hawkins." He shakes his head. "God." He chuckles.

"I'm so sorry," she apologizes. "Oh my gosh."

"I've heard worse," he dismisses her.

"I'm never living that down, am I?" She hides her face in his neck. "I can't believe I said that out loud. That's so embarrassing."

"No. I'll remind you of it until we're gray and old," he murmurs into her hair. He says the words with so much conviction. Like he believes them. Like he wants those words to be true.

"You plan on sticking around that long, huh?"

"Maybe," he shrugs. "Depends on if you want me to."

He sounds so hesitant. And it's only within that moment that Nova realizes Atlas isn't used to this. To be wanted by someone.

"As long as you'll let me," she responds.

And for a second, he believes her.

"You'll get tired of me eventually, Wrenning Bird."

"Doubt it."

There's a brief lapse of silence before either of them speaks again.

"What is this?" Nova asks, suddenly, hesitantly.

There's something different, something so much more.

"I don't know," Atlas admits truthfully. "Is that okay?"

Nova ponders for a moment. "Yeah." She nods "That's okay."

"You're my Wrenning Bird." He says it with so much emotion.

"Is that enough?" She wonders aloud.

"It is to me—you're more than enough."

"Then it's enough for me too."

The moon seems to hang low in the night, beneath autumn skies and stratus clouds—there is Atlas and his Wrenning Bird. There is Nova and her moon. Beneath the evening autumn skies and the slight murmuring song of Nightjar birds—there is Atlas and Nova. And for once, for a second, for this lapsed moment, they are enough.

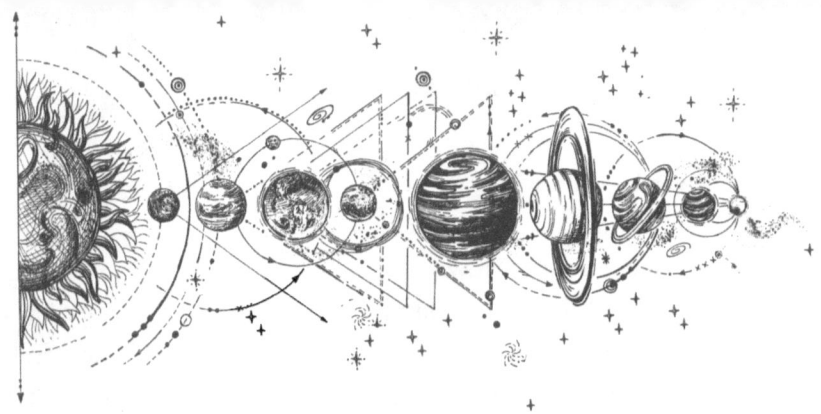

chapter nineteen.
bluebird song

Atlas likes to compare Nova's voice to the sound of bluebirds singing. Something that resembles a low-pitched hum during an evening rain. He likes to think about her voice, how it reminds him of the lullaby that his mother once sang to him when he was a small boy. She reminds him of home, which is odd because his entire life he believed that home was a place. But instead, it is a person. Perhaps it would one day be Nova.

"Do you want to talk about it?" he asks her from his place on the bed. Atlas watches as she reaches up on her toes to open the curtains.

"No." She shrugs. "I like what we are."

Though neither is entirely sure what that even is.

Last night was a turning point, something that will shift their relationship for the rest of the foreseeable future.

"Me too," he agrees.

She looks radiant among the sun like she belongs to it.

Nova watches him with careful eyes. "You're thinking again."

"When am I not thinking?" Atlas snorts.

"Atlas." She raises her brow.

"People in my life have a habit of leaving. I like how we are now. I like that I can talk to you about anything and everything. How it feels like no time has passed whenever I'm with you, even if hours have." He feels the bed dip beside him. "I don't ever want to wake up and not have you in my life," Atlas admits. "Alot has changed these past few months but you're the only thing that has been constant. I think I like who we are right now—us, the people we are when we're together."

"I like that too." She interlaces their hands. "Nothing has to change. For once, we are entirely in control of our lives. We can just be this. Atlas and Nova. Nothing more, and nothing less."

"Is that what *you* want?" He glances down at their hands.

A crease appears on her brow. "I want whatever you want."

"What if I don't know what that is?"

"Then we'll be confused together."

Atlas lets out a small chuckle and shakes his head. "You have an answer for everything, huh?" But of course, she does; she's Nova.

"Of course," she says, as though she's read his mind.

Groaning, Atlas allows himself to fall back on the bed, taking the smaller brunette down with him. He feels his head hit the pillow and sighs, shaking his head to himself. "How did we even get here?"

"Well," Nova says, "if I remember correctly, I was visiting the park for my mom's anniversary. I think I was feeling a bit nostalgic, honestly. Anyway, I was trying to enjoy the silence when all of a sudden, this random brooding man interrupted my day of peace."

His eyes crack open. "It's a public place."

"Shh." She brushes him off. "I'm trying to tell a story."

"My apologies," he murmurs in his amusement.

"Anyway, this random dude comes out of nowhere and decides to smoke right next to me—which is disgusting, by the way."

"You want me to stop?"

Nova pauses. "Would you actually?"

"Nah." Atlas smirks.

Rolling her eyes, Nova continues, "And then the rest is history."

"You forgot the part where you practically blackmailed me into being friends with you."

"I did *not* blackmail you. Besides, I didn't see you again for two months and then another two weeks after that. And then, when we finally hung out that day at the café, you literally disappeared—*again*, for a week. I deserve compensation for the number of times you ignored me. You need to be happy that I even wanted to talk to you again after that."

"I'm glad you decided to give me another chance."

She finds herself smiling at that. "Yeah. Me too."

"What happens when the bucket list is done? What then? Do we just move on from this like nothing ever even happened?"

"I'm not going to pretend to know where the future is headed. But I do know that whatever it is that I feel for you is real. I know that when I'm with you, it feels like flying; ever since the first day I met you in the park, conversation has never been hard for us. And I know that I've never had that before in my life. Right now, that's enough for me."

"I've never had stability, ever. That's never been a thing for me. But you're constant. You've never left. Not yet, at least. But I like that I don't have to worry about you disappearing or not wanting to be around. But I flake a lot when things get hard. I need you to know that. Sometimes I leave because it's the best that I can do. It's all I know."

"Then I'll be here. Whenever you decide to show up again."

"Sometimes I think that you make me feel like I'm not broken. Like

I don't wake up in the night screaming—or like I'm not left behind. From the moment I met you, you've never looked at me like I wasn't normal. I've only had a few people look at me like that in my life."

Nova sits up slowly, peering down at him. "You're not broken."

"I thought we were all a little broken." He repeats her words from the previous day, a slight smile on his face. "I'm all right, promise."

"And you'll tell me—if you ever feel like you're not. You'll tell me, right? Whenever you are going through something, you tell me."

There's a look in her eyes, the kind of look that Catie gives him when he forgets to eat; when he shuts down sometimes and shows up in the same clothes he's been wearing for the past few days. It's not pity, more like faint sadness—slight fear. So Atlas sighs and nods. He pulls her close until her head rests under his chin, and he lies. He simply lies because his trauma and his baggage are no less Nova's problem than anyone else's. His pain is for him to deal with, to cope with alone.

"I don't believe much in God," he murmurs into her hair, "I've never cared much for the philosophy of religion." His lips press softly against her temple, trailing whisper-riddled kisses across her forehead, "But you, Nova Hawkins, have somehow managed to exemplify the heavens. If there is a God, which there must be, then I think he lives so deep within you that his love shines from you and out into the world."

"Belief is faulty anyway."

"I believe in you—that there is some type of good in the world. You show me that; you've shown me that from that day in the park, at the café, and again at Murray's. You are good. You're so good it hurts."

"You're good too. Even if you wish to hide it. You're as good as anyone gets Atlas."

"Mm," Atlas grunts. "Agree to disagree."

Nova merely shakes her head and wraps her arms tightly around his waist. "Thanks for showing up that night in the park."

Sometimes Atlas wonders how different these past few months would have been had he never gone to the park that night. He wonders if he would have ever run into Nova on his own without it. Were they simply fated to meet, always? Or was this simply a chance encounter?

"Thanks for deciding to stay when I did," he mumbles.

"I think we would've always found each other," Nova says as if plucking the thought from his head and answering it. "We would've always ended up as friends; would've somehow ended up here. I think that fate is real. That's what I believe in, anyway. We're born with this unique life, this one chance opportunity to do good in the world. And somewhere along the way, our paths are fated to cross with someone else's. I think we were always going to meet Hale. *It was written in the stars,* woooo." She ends in a mysterious voice, wiggling her fingers,

Snorting, Atlas pushes her away. "That was extremely cheesy, even for you, Hawkins."

"Whatever," she grumbles, climbing off the bed. "You get my point, though. We would've met now or in a million years. You can't get rid of me that easily, Atlas Hale. You're stuck with me forever."

"Forever, huh?" He raises his brow. "Long time."

"Well, I'm young—what can I say?" She shrugs as she gathers her clothes in her hands. "I'm going to get dressed. See you out there?"

Atlas watches her hopeful eyes. She's asking so much without even saying much of anything. She wants to know that nothing will change when they walk down there. That they'll still be them.

"Yeah," he says, "I'll see you down there."

And her smile is enough for him.

Sometimes, the mere thought of her is enough to scare him. Because Nova is so different. She's so completely her own that it terrifies him. Nova doesn't lean on him in the ways that he does with her. She's so secure and reassured in herself, so completely at ease in her own skin.

She wears her mismatched Converses and brightly colored sweaters, never once thinking about how others may view her. She doesn't worry about tomorrow; she simply knows that it will be there. But Atlas, that will never be him. He's meticulous—sought out. He checks the weather at the same time every day, and his shoes are perfectly white. His clothes are pressed thin, never wrinkled or out of place. He wears his watch on his left wrist and never the right. He cares about tomorrow because they're never guaranteed for him. He is not colorful; his art is bland—black and gray. That is who Atlas is. Where Nova is sunshine, he is dark. Where she speaks her mind with ease, he is utterly reserved.

They are night and day, Nova and Atlas. And it terrifies him.

Sometimes, Nova reminds Atlas of home. And it terrifies him.

Because home had always felt safe until it wasn't.

Home had once been happy and constant until it wasn't.

Atlas had never had the best luck in life; his mother had left, and his father had all but abandoned him shortly after. Everyone he had ever cared about had left with the rise and fall of the sun and disappeared right before his eyes.

"Atlas?" She peeks her head into the room, "Are you coming?"

Sometimes, Nova reminds Atlas of home.

Her smile is bright, so promising. But so was home once.

Until it wasn't.

"Yeah." His smile is tight. "Yeah, I'm coming."

PART THREE,
the fulfillment of love.

chapter twenty.
my love is mine all mine

Atlas had never believed in love, not much. Not before Nova, at least. He had never given much thought to the intricacy of it—the art of it. It was the last thing that had ever been on his mind in the time that passed before her. But when he did think about it, he sometimes wondered what it would be like to fall in love. It was embarrassing—when he thinks back on it—how truly out of touch he had been with the world; how poorly he had viewed it once. He remembers referring to the world as a cesspool; some type of continuous sinkhole that eventually drowned you in nothing but quiet sorrows. But that all changed when he met Nova. He figures it's cliché; the idea that one person had the inmate power to utterly shift your worldview, and it is. But that was what had happened. At times, he can pinpoint the exact moment when he realized friendship was out of the picture for them. He knows the exact millisecond.

It was the day he had held her when he realized he had been afraid when he received the call from Indie. When he realized how sad it had made him that she was alone in the park somewhere, crying.

It had been that day, in the backyard of his mother's home, that he realized how much he cherished their conversations—and how sacred they had become to him in such a short time. He always hated the idea of instant attraction, but he wasn't stupid. He found Nova attractive from the moment that he saw her that day in the park. She had looked beautiful—odd, in her brightly colored shoes—but beautiful, nonetheless.

He can remember wanting to walk her home—wanting to hold her hand. Atlas can vividly pinpoint the exact second that the smile on her face became something so close to a drug that it began to scare him. He thinks back to the first conversation that they had, about the stars, and he can't help but shake his head. He nearly scoffs at the thought.

"You're drifting off again." Her voice is like a beacon. "You haven't heard a singular word I've said this entire time."

They're at the park—not as much of a coincidence as he wishes it had been but, besides the point—the ground is covered in dull, lifeless leaves. So vastly different from the first night they had been here.

"I heard enough." He shrugs, turning his head to peer down at her.

"We're going to get hyperthermia out here," Nova chastises him. "We should be at the festival right now, anyway. You know this is the first year that I've not gone? You're a horrible influence."

"Live a little, Hawkins." He finds himself smirking.

She purses her lips and rolls her eyes.

The annual harvest festival has been a staple in Sailor Ridge for years; held every year to commemorate the ending of fall, the festival was used as a fundraising effort for the townsfolk. This year, the proceeds would all go toward the gymnasium for the local elementary school.

"What are we doing here, anyway?"

"Is it so odd that I wanted to spend time with you?"

It's a lie, a bad one, but he's too nervous to think of anything else.

His mind has been preoccupied so much with Nova in the days that followed after her bedroom. She has become a tethered thought that protruded from his mind long before he even awakened. He wants to say so much, but can't muster it quite well enough. He wants to tell her how he feels, that his thoughts belong to her—that he doesn't want the bucket list to be the end of them. And that none of this has gone as planned.

He wishes to tell her that he is wrecked—completely, and utterly wrecked in contemplation of her. And that there are moments when he feels as though he cannot function without her near.

"No—I would just rather not do it when it's freezing outside."

Her breaths are visible in the air, and he starts to feel bad.

"We can go back to your place, or mine. Get out of the cold. Sorry, this was stupid, wasn't it? Come on. We can leave."

"Atlas." Nova reaches for him. "What are we doing here?"

"Do you think that love is real?" he asks randomly, ignoring her question. "Do you think that it's worth it if it is real?"

Furrowing her brow, Nova pushes herself up on her elbows. "Yes." She answers truthfully, "Yes, to both of those questions." She wipes her dampening hands on her jeans. "I think that love is the purest thing that we could ever do and I think that if we come across love with someone, then we should hold on to it for as long as we possibly can."

"How do you know when you're in love with someone?"

His question causes a blanket of silence to fall over them, and he suddenly begins to dread his words. As he moves to take them back, Nova takes his hand in her own. They're cold, much like the first time.

"I don't know. As embarrassing as it is, I've spent the past twenty-one years of my life never being in love with anyone. I don't know much about love—not much at all other than the stuff that I read in books and see in movies. My mom used to tell me that there was an art to falling in love. That it was something intricate and thought out. And that it happens when you least expect it but, you'll know when it's real."

"That's stupid." Atlas covers his nervousness with a feigned laugh. It's so obviously forced, so faint. His voice is so hesitant.

"Extremely stupid," Nova agrees, leaning her head against his shoulder. "There should be an instruction manual or something," she jokes. "A how-to for dummies who have never been in love."

He pauses for a moment, briefly. It takes him a moment, but when he speaks again, he says, "I think I could love you one day, eventually." He admits; to her, the trees, the grass, and anyone else who could listen.

She picks her head up to look at him. And her eyes are tinged with promise—understanding and hope. "I'm not going anywhere."

"I know," he replies. "I just wanted to let you know."

Her smile is so small, but it says so much. "Tell me again tomorrow," she tells him. "I like who we are now," Nova repeats her words from days before. "There's no rush, you know?"

"But one day, you could see it too, right?"

She presses a kiss to his cheek, before pulling back and saying, "Yeah. I could. But for now, we're us. Just—Atlas and Nova."

"Yeah," he agrees.

She glances down at her interlaced hands, and smiles again. "Where's the one place you've always wanted to go?" she asks.

"Antarctica." He shrugs, causing her to deadpan. "You?"

"To the moon," she admits quietly. There is momentary silence; lingering, intruding. "I'm going to take you to the moon one day, Atlas Hale," Nova promises like she believes it'll happen.

He never gave much thought to love—not before Nova. But when he is with her, he can see it. He can see love. In her eyes, in her smile, in the soft touch that drifted down his forearm; Altas can see it, and for once, he finds himself wanting it one day.

"I think I'd like that." To Nova, the moon is infinite. "I think that I would like that a lot." And an infinity with Nova doesn't seem so bad. "Just you and me, Hawkins. To the moon?"

She holds up her pinky at his words, and he nearly groans at the sight. Shaking his head, Atlas hooks his pinky around her own.

"*To the moon.*" Nova nods.

chapter twenty-one
speedways, happy feet, and hi's
(play orange show speedway by lizzy mcalpine)

She likes to think that she fell for him truly that day at the Speedway. The random Speedway on the corner of the Harpersburg, near the turnoff, sat among deserted lands and random trailer homes. It was the side of town that most people never visited more than once unless they had to. Nova likes to believe that her feelings became far more evident to him that day. She thinks that he realized the vast realness of her emotions during that trip. Beneath the autumn skies and shared cherry cola slushies, Nova likes to think that was when she fell the hardest for Atlas Hale. She remembers the way that his hair looked—how distinctly out of place it was that one random afternoon. She remembers how his cheeks flushed from the cold, how his deep laugh mixed with the wind.

She specifically remembers the color shirt he was wearing and how

his lips felt against her own—how cold they were from the lingering remnants of the ice-cold drink on his lips. She remembers the laughter that echoed afterward and how content they were in that moment.

She remembers thinking that, perhaps, this was truly more. No kiss had ever felt like that—*tasted* like that. It had been so perfectly imperfect. It was so them. Broken, filled with sighs and stares of longing. It was perfect. So perfect that she did it again, and again, and again. Simply because she could. Kissing him felt like falling.

She thinks that's when she fell in love with him—under the orange, red fluorescent lights of the random Harpersburg Speedway.

"My mom used to bring me here, at least once a week," Nova tells him as they walk out of the nearly empty gas station. "She would get a large big gulp for the two of us to share and we would sit in the backseat of the car watching movies on the old television." She gestures with her fingers. "You know the ones that you could hang on the headrest?" Her laughter echoes across the space. "Anyway, we would sit in the back with blankets and watch Happy Feet on an old skipping CD."

"Sounds like you were living the dream." Atlas smirks, holding his hand out for the cup. She had opted for two straws instead.

"Yeah." She smiles softly to herself. "I miss her."

"I know."

"Sometimes I hate talking about her. It's like even though the memories are good, they still hurt. It feels like I would rather remember the bad memories with her instead—maybe it won't hurt so bad." She stirs absentmindedly. "Here"—she hands him the cup—"I think I'm done."

Atlas notes that she gets like this a lot when she talks about her mom. Almost as though the world is weighing down on her; like it refuses to give her a hint of a slight reprieve. But he understands. He knows far more than anyone should how it feels to miss a parent.

They approach the truck at a slow pace—their feet dragging. The day has flown by so quickly. The months have passed with such an unforgiving amount of speed that they can hardly even keep up.

"Thank you for bringing me here," she says once they're inside. "I've been meaning to come here for a while, but I was nervous to do it alone. So thank you seriously. I mean, for everything you've done."

"You've done things for me, too. Far more than I can count. I think I owe you way more than just a ride into the next town over."

"This isn't a competition. We're here for each other." She holds his hand over the armrest. "That's what we do, who we are."

They're two souls wandering, searching for a place to call home, and somewhere along the way they had found it among each other.

"You were unpredictable. I don't think that I could have ever predicted someone like you, Nova. But the best things in life come unexpectedly. If I could go back in time and meet you all over again, I would do it in a heartbeat. I don't want to lose this—us."

"We're an *us* now, huh?" Nova can't contain the slight smile that arose on her face. "I like the sound of that."

"Maybe. We could be if you want?"

"Geez, ask me on a date first, would you?"

"Okay," he says with ease.

"What?" She lets out a breathy laugh.

"Okay." He turns to face her. "Let's go on a date."

Raising her brow, Nova pulls back to look at him. "Right now?"

"Yeah, why not?" He shrugs.

"Here—at some crusty gas station?" She glances around, taking the loitering strangers and the stray dogs wandering around. It's not perfect, or pretty. It's by no means done up or remotely clean but, it's them. Chipped and worn a bit rough around the edges and broken, "Okay." She nods, much to his surprise. "Yeah, let's do it."

His smile is slow and steady—lazy. "Yeah?"

"Yeah. I couldn't think of anything more perfect."

She remembers the first date she had ever been on; it had been with John Eaton from sophomore year of university. He had gone out of his way to buy her favorite flowers and to ensure that he had gotten her the best chocolates. It had all been so annoyingly overdone and almost fabricated. There was no spark—no thrill or actual conversation. But not with Atlas. Everything felt natural, as smooth and as simple as breathing.

"There's a blanket in the back. We can sit there, and watch *Happy Feet*." He watches her smile grow, biting back his own when she places a kiss on his cheek. "I'll take that as a yes, then?"

It's such a small thing—so minuscule. It's even more so particularly childish, but to Nova, it is perfect. They sit in the backseat of the truck, a wool blanket spread across them with only the light from the orange-yellow lamps above and his phone illuminating the space. Her head rests against his shoulder and every now and then, laughter erupts from them. The moment is so pure, so intimate.

They sit there, and among the autumn skies, it feels like heartbeats are pulsating in the air. Tendrils, and soft murmurs—everything is tied to this moment. His hand rests on her thigh, and her free hand runs in soothing circles down his arm. His words are muffled, the chatter from his phone drowning it out, but she can hear it. He's whispering in her ear, not paying much attention to the scenes and animations. Atlas tells her stories about his childhood—his memories—and soon the movie is long forgotten. She always assumed relationships had to be more; that they had to be far more physical to have meaning. But conversations with Atlas made her feel naked. Like she was exposed down to the tips of her fingers; completely at his disposal. Laid out for him to view.

"I remember," he chuckles softly, "the first time I got caught in the back of Mr. Hawthorne's truck." He shakes his head like the memory is foolish. "I thought he would be upset, but all he did was throw me some condoms and tell me to wrap it up before he became a grandpa."

She laughs alongside him. "You have a lot of random rendezvous?"

"Nah." His lips tip up. "Unless you count this one."

"Barely a rendezvous if there's no kissing."

"You askin' me to kiss you, Hawkins?"

Say it—she thinks to herself—*gosh, say it*.

"Maybe." She gnaws on her bottom lip. "I mean, if you want?"

His phone screen illuminates the darkened space, and shadows are cast against the walls of the truck—there's this electrifying current pushing, and Nova swears she can hear her heart beating alongside the silence. His hand tightens against her thigh, and her eyes are trained to it because she cannot will herself to look him in the eye. There's an odd rendition of *Heartbreak Hotel* playing softly in the back, and a homeless man yelling at a stray dog fills the air alongside it. She can feel his heartbeat in his fingertips—it's erratic, jumbled, much like her own emotions.

"Breathe," she whispers, with a choked laugh interlacing their fingers. "I can feel your heart beating." Nova tucks a stray hair behind her ear. "It was just a question—stupid, I guess. I shouldn't have even asked."

"Nova," he whispers her name like it's a prayer. With so much conviction—so much love, and care that she closes her eyes to relish in the sound. She wants to take hold of the syllables. "You can't just say stuff like that to me if you don't mean it," Atlas rasps.

His free hand tips her chin up until their eyes are locked; his are darkened, morphing the lines of an icy gray—her own are widened, training on his lips. She wants to kiss him. She craves it religiously.

"Kiss me," she whispers, though it's nearly close to a whimper. She's tugging softly at his shirt now, and her breaths are coming out in bursts. She can't speak. She doesn't know what to say. It's like her brain doesn't know how to function or compute, or anything. Nothing comes out. But she wants him. God, she wants him to kiss her. To consume her.

She wonders how they got here; she wonders when it changed.

"Everything will change." His hand cradles the back of her neck, tugging softly at the curls forming at her neck. "Tell me it's okay." He begs, "Tell me that we'll still be us after this. I *can't* lose you."

"We're us—just us. That's okay," she reassures him. "I promise." Her forehead brushes against his own. "It's okay. Kiss me, please."

He lets out a haunted groan before his lips collide with hers. He kisses her fervently like there is an ocean length of time written between their two lips. He kisses her as though to worship her through sighs, and heavy breaths; he's tethered to the softened gasps that escape her mouth. Atlas kisses her with passion as though she might slip from his embrace and this kiss would be their ruination. He kisses her as though the world might succumb, shatter, and cease to exist. Atlas kisses her, and he feels like he's falling. But for once, someone will catch him.

Nova will catch him. And for once, he isn't afraid anymore.

When he pulls away, they're both breathless, and as he leans his forehead against her own—he lets out a huffed laugh. "Fuck."

She can't contain her burst of giggles alongside him.

Their giggles filled the back of the truck, alongside the soft melodies of Elvis. They laugh and laugh, and laugh. It is perfect.

She realizes in that moment as she watches his cheeks flush and turn a darkening color of red; as she watches the crinkles by his eyes because his smile is beginning to overtake his entire face, Nova knows. Beneath the orange-yellow fluorescent lights, half-drunken Cherry Coke slushies, late autumn skies, and the occasional homeless man— Nova realizes that what she feels is the simplest form of what love could eventually be. It is the chemtrails, the beginning hidden beneath fluttered lashes, and half-moon smiles. This alone is love in its simplest form.

She loves him broken, she loves him shattered. Nova is falling in love with the fragments of him—the shards that seem to poke and pierce the skin. She is falling in love with the parts of him that are dirtied and messy. Nova falls in love with his mind, which seems to be most unkind to him. Atlas Hale was sudden; he appeared in her darkest of times and even though he is shrouded in pain, he has somehow managed to become her light. He is everything.

"Hi," he whispers. His hand is warm as it cups her cheeks.

"Hi—hi, Atlas." Her smile is so soft, so filled with contentment.

He presses a kiss to the inside of her palm and he sits so close that his breath fans out in puffs along her cheek. "I fear I am completely mesmerized by you." His brow furrows. It's endearing, and his gaze softens. "I have become accustomed to your warmth." Atlas traces the space above her heart. "You're perfect, Nova."

She kisses him again, chasing after the high that seems to be hung from his lips. His fingers tangle in her hair, tugging and pulling with every shattered gasp. She only pulls away to smile. "Hi," she whispers.

He hums softly. "Hi, baby."

She nods. "I like it." Her cheeks darken.

"Yeah?" Atlas' grin widens.

"*Yeah.*"

"You and me?" He holds his pinky up. It's childish, but he doesn't care. "I like who we are now. I don't ever wanna wake up and not have you in my life. So promise me, Nova, that it's us for as long as we can keep it that way. That we'll be us until something tears us apart."

It was a big ask, and maybe they were both too drunk on the high from their kiss to even weigh the consequences. But love is cloudy, and is a haze filled with lavender, and trails of red. Love is blinding. It is something that consumes you completely until you see nothing else, until you see no end. So she smiles and says, *"Promise."*

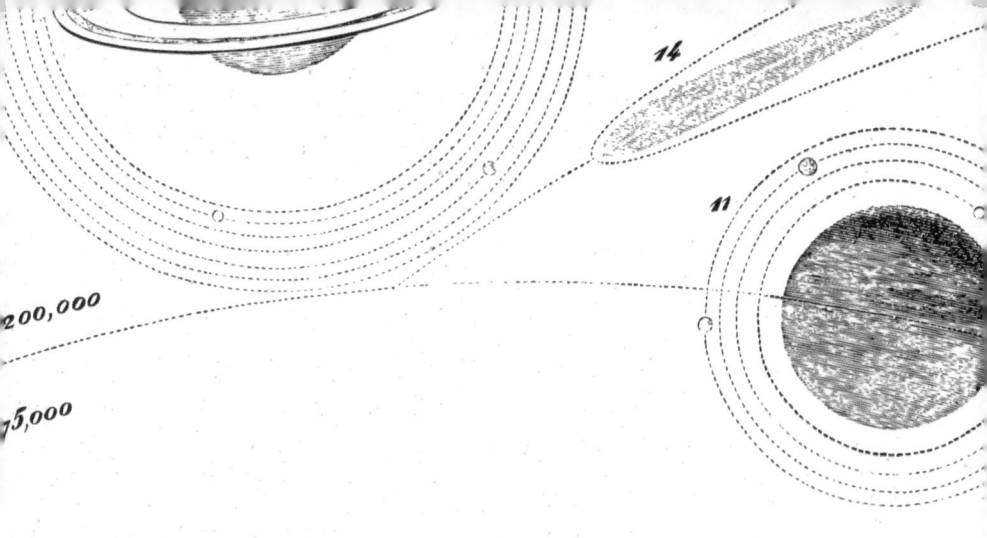

INTERLUDE.
chemtrails

Love is like a chemtrail, in that it is mysterious.[1] An odd phenomenon that occurs at random—so suddenly that there is hardly an explanation. It is a paradox, something from medieval times. Scientists have attempted to dissect it; to pick and pull it apart but love, well, it is written in the stars. It is something fated even before one is born. Love is entailed with consequences, weaved and woven like string. Love is like a chemtrail in that it is a mystery. No one quite knows why it happens—there are conspiracies about it, about the whys and hows of it. But when it happens, it is something no one can quite fathom.
Love is a chemtrail—visible, tangible, and coated in the air.

---

[1] Chemtrail, a visible trail left in the sky by an aircraft and believed by some to consist of chemical or biological agents released as part of a covert operation.

chapter twenty-two
adoration, and harry's garage.

Atlas never thought that he would experience utter adoration until he looks at her, *really* looks at her, and it feels as though light will descend and grace her face. He is well aware of the dangers that can come from idolizing and giving an almost divine association to someone—to make a human so utterly close to God. But, sometimes, Atlas sees her and his entire day no matter how filled with disappointments and pain that it might be, becomes better.

Nova makes him feel *hope*. Hope. It is a word used to describe the feeling of expectation, or searching; desire. The word is commonly used in a far more positive manner, though Atlas once could not see it as such. Hope is tethered, in Atlas's eyes, to pain. In his vocabulary, the word had once been surrounded by similarities fueled by nothing but falsities. But Nova makes him feel hope. Hope is littered across her eyes when she looks at him alongside something else that he doesn't quite want to dissect at the moment. When she looks at him, he feels seen

and heard. He feels like his problems (if only for a second) manage to disappear; when he is with her, there is a short reprieve.

"You want a beer or something, man?" Micah's voice breaks through his thoughts. "Guinness, or Corona?" He holds up the glasses.

"Guinness," Parker answers for him from his place against the couch. "Corona tastes like you licked piss off a sidewalk." He gags.

The two men pause, turning to look at him.

"What?" Parker looks between them. "It's true."

Micah shakes his head, mutters, "You're fucking stupid."

Parker merely shrugs, snagging the bottle from his hand.

"Atlas," Micah calls again. "Beer?"

"Nah, man," he declines. "M'good."

"Since when do you not drink beer?" Parker snorts.

"Since today. I'm just not in the mood."

Narrowing his eyes, Micah places a cool hand on his friend's forehead. "You don't look sick." He squishes his face. "You okay?"

Atlas scoffs, slapping his hand away. "Get off me, idiot."

"Maybe he's sex deprived. I would be depressed too." Parker chimes in, "You poor horny bastard." He sniffles, feigning tears.

"I don't need to get laid," Atlas grumbles.

"Kind of hard to do when he's in love," Damien grunts as he slides out from under the car he's been working on. "What?" He shrugs, dusting his hands off. "Don't give me that look—you're in love."

They're gathered in the old garage downtown. Atlas and Damien have been coming here since they were teenagers, messing around and getting on old man Harry's nerves any chance they could get. Damien has been working at the garage since he turned eighteen and finally bought it out early last year when Harry became too sickly to keep it up. When he passed away earlier this year, Damien simply didn't have the heart to change the name. *This place belonged to Harry*, he said.

Damien has always been handy with a wrench as opposed to Atlas, who seeks solace in his paints and photography. The rest of their ragtag group of friends seems to migrate here as well on the weekends; popping beers and watching the game on the busted couch whenever the shop closes down. For the time being, Damien is working on a busted Toyota Pruis from old man Harriss a few blocks over.

"You're obsessed." Damien shrugs.

"I'm not obsessed," Atlas shoots back.

Damien snorts. "Whatever you say, man."

"I think it's kind of endearing." Parker shrugs.

"Of course you do." Micah rolls his eyes.

"Look." Damien sighs. "In all seriousness, this is the happiest you've been in a while. We're happy for you. You deserve it more than any of us." He raises his beer. "Don't fuck it up."

"Yeah. You deserve it, even if it turns you into a lovesick emo."

"I'm leaving," Atlas grumbles, standing. "Goodbye."

"Oh, come on, man. We're just joking," Parker calls after him.

"*So whipped*," Damien mutters.

Atlas flips them off over his shoulder, though he can't seem to contain his slight smile. If he is whipped, so be it. He is happy. For once, happiness lasts for more than a few days.

When he sees her again for the first time after their kiss that night, Atlas feels a nervousness he wasn't even aware could resonate within him. His palms are sweating profusely and he's run his fingers through his hair so many times he's convinced he's dug a bald spot. He stands leaning against his truck, fidgeting with the end of his flannel when he sees her. She rushed toward him, her thin white skirt blowing in the evening wind. Her hair is pulled into space buns and her feet are covered by Doc Martens with ribbons instead of the regular laces. Atlas can't contain the smile that rises on his face; she's sunshine—springtime in a person. When she approaches him, her arms latch around his neck instantly and he feels like he's returned home after some type of war.

She smells of lilies and lilacs—a hint of spice, same as always.

"Hi," she murmurs into his neck.

"Missed you." He holds her as close as he can.

It's been a day, but every second away from her feels like torture.

"Missed you," she replies softly.

Atlas hums, kissing her forehead. "Good day?"

"Best day." Nova grins.

"You hungry? I was going to swing by Connie's before I dropped you off at home. We can go somewhere else if you want."

She shakes her head and presses a kiss to his cheek. "It's perfect."

He snags her bag from her hand, lifting it onto his shoulder. "Got a question," Atlas says as they begin their walk over to Connies.

"Hm?"

"Micah's looking for someone to look after Delly for a few weeks. His nanny is going out of town for the holidays. I was wondering if maybe Indie or Sienna would be interested in some extra cash?"

"Indie just started her job at the inn, so she's going to be pretty busy. Sienna though, uh." Nova winces, "Not sure she's the best influence to be around a three-year-old. She curses like a sailor."

Atlas chuckles, nodding. "Yeah, maybe not Sienna."

"No, definitely not." She laughs. "But hey, I'll ask around."

He presses a kiss to her temple. "Thanks," he murmurs.

"Oh! Also…" She turns she's facing him. "Speaking of the holidays. I was wondering if you had any plans. Normally, we throw this ugly sweater party—and by party, I mean it's me, Indie, and Sienna dressed up in atrocious sweaters watching Christmas movies—on Christmas Eve every year. I wanted to know if you maybe wanted to come. You can invite the guys, of course." She searches his eyes. "Or–*or* not, you definitely don't have to do that at all." Nova furrows her brow. "Sorry."

"I don't usually celebrate the holidays much." Atlas clears his throat. "I normally just eat dinner with Murray, and that's all."

"Oh, well, Murray is welcome to come too if he wants—"

"—Maybe next year, yeah?" he interjects.

Her face falls at his words, but she recovers quickly. "Yeah."

His brow pinches as he takes in her dejected tone. "Nova."

"It's *fine*," she lies. "We all have our things."

"Nova." He reaches for her.

"M'gonna go order of us, okay?" She sends him a small smile.

Shit, he thinks.

The ride back to her apartment is oddly silent. It's the deafening kind that makes you want to scratch your eyes out and scream just to hear something—anything. He keeps peeking at her from the corner of his eye, hoping that she'll glance over at him and say something, but she never does. She sits with her shoes off and her knees to her chest. The setting sun is hitting her skin just right, and Atlas can't help but watch. He watches as Nova perches her chin against the window rest, as the brisk winter air sends her hair flying in flurries around her. Atlas watches as contentment and a mixture of disdain seem to settle in the very marrow of her bones, and how the scent of winter passing causes her cheeks to rise. The heat is blowing harshly from the vents, and her nail polish is chipped. There's a creak in his truck, but even in the utter silence, even when he's sure that she's upset with him—Atlas watches. He watched, and he watched because Atlas had always been captivated by beautiful things. Because Nova Hawkins was breathtakingly beautiful.

"Staring is creepy," Nova comments, making his cheeks flush.

"M'sorry," he mumbles.

"It's okay."

There's more silence again.

"It's important to me," she says randomly.

"I'm sorry?" He turns down the heat to hear her better.

"The sweaters." She picks at her nails. "It's stupid, I know. But it was the one thing that my mom did every year. She would"—she shakes her head at the memory—"go to Walmart and find the most atrocious sweaters and she would force me to wear them. We would go with Indie and her mother around the neighborhood and look at the Christmas lights. It was the smallest, most simple thing, but it was important to her. So I've done it the past two years since she died," Nova finishes.

Atlas swallows harshly. "Thank you for telling me," he musters out. "I'm sorry that I shut you down so quickly but the holidays aren't the best time for me. They never have been. It's hard to be happy and to celebrate something when I have *nothing*. I get it—I know why you do it. But I can't do it. Not this year. I'm sorry."

"You have me?" She sends him an uncertain smile.

He reaches over with his free hand to trace her jaw. His hands are cold from the air outside but she embraces the touch anyway. "S'not what I meant but—I know. I know that I have you now."

"For as long as you'll let me." She nods.

"Don't be upset if I keep you here forever," he jokes.

"What are you going to do, kidnap me?"

He snorts. "Please, Hawkins, I wouldn't have to kidnap you."

She rolls her eyes. "Whatever."

The car shifts as they turn down the winding road. The leaves are an umber brown, and the skyline is foggy. Winter seems to have crept in unannounced, without a single warning to anyone at all.

"You and me?" he speaks out in the silence.

"*You and me,*" Nova whispers.

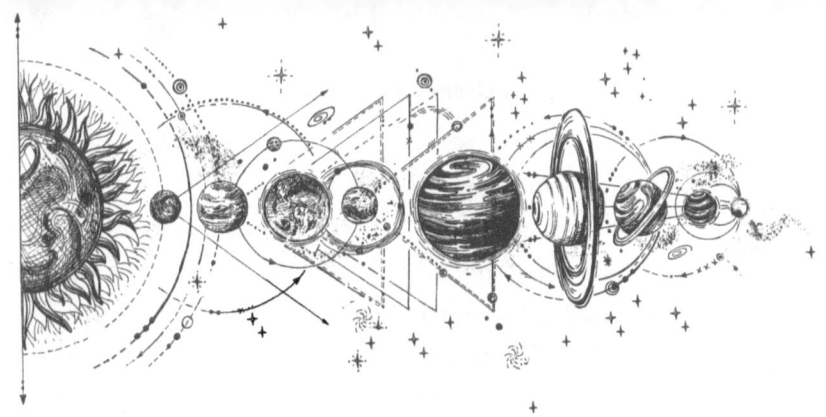

chapter twenty-three
you are a vesper

Nova dreads nothing more than her birthday. Growing up, the day had been joyous, filled with laughter, and a sense of satisfaction at another passing year, and now—it is filled with nothing but dread and heartache. Soon after her mother died, Nova received a letter alongside a box in the mail addressed to her from her deceased mother. She remembers the day as though it were mere moments ago; the acute amount of pain that filled her chest, the anger, and the bout of loneliness that followed. She took the box and hid it in the back of her closet until a few months ago, when she finally worked up the courage to unveil the contents. There were pictures—all polaroids—that she hadn't even been aware her mother had taken of her. In most, Nova looks happy–*free*. In others, there is a slight tiredness in her eyes. She can tell based on the photographs the exact time and year it was. The closer in date it became to the day of her mother's passing, the more tired her eyes appeared.

Alongside the pictures were letters—dated back to the day her mother was first diagnosed with cancer. The letters start with the number twelve and end at around sixty. Her mother wrote a singular letter for every birthday Nova will have up until the age of fifty. One letter for every birthday Marjorie will miss. Nova hasn't opened them—she is far too afraid to. She finds herself in pain at the thought of her mother knowing that she would die or at least having some type of reconciliation with her eventual death.

Today is her birthday. She is turning twenty-two, and as she stares down at the satin box in her hand—Nova feels as though her heart is being ripped out of her chest and carved out by a paring knife. She hears a soft knock at her bedroom door and lets out a shaky breath. "Come in."

"Hey." Indie, it is always Indie. "I bought you coffee."

Nova sends the ebony-haired girl a slight smile. "Thanks."

Indie crosses the room, placing the cup on Nova's desk. "Marjorie." She shakes her head. "Always so whimsical." Indie runs her hand along the brim of the box. "You don't have to open it today."

"It's been two years." Nova runs a tired hand down her face. "If I keep putting it off, I'll never open any of them. And I don't want to hurt her like that, you know? She made them for a reason. It's all that I have left of her; of her thoughts, of her dreams—all of it."

"Do you want me to be there with you?"

"No," Nova says, despite the tremble in her voice.

"Maggie." Indie grasps her hand. "It's you and me against the world. It always has been. You know that. I'm here if you need me."

"I know." And she does. Because Indie is her person in all the ways that counts. Her mother used to say that they were soulmates.

"Happy Birthday," Indie whispers softly, before leaving the brunette to her thoughts.

How fair is it that Nova gets to celebrate birthdays and live when her mother never had a chance to? *Life was a sick joke.*

"Guess who?" Her eyesight is obscured by a warm hand.

"Hm," Nova pretends to ponder for a moment. "Parker?"

"Cheeky," Atlas mumbles, pulling her into a hug. "Happy birthday, baby," he murmurs into her hair. "You okay?" he asks once they've pulled away. Her smile is tired, and her eyes are bloodshot.

"Mm," is all that she can muster.

"We don't have to do this, you know?" he attempts to sway her. "Seriously, we can ditch the cookout and eat at your place."

She shakes her head. "No. Besides, I'm starving and your mom makes those crinkle fries that I like." Their arms swing in communion with each other. "That and everyone is here, anyway. It's rude to bail."

Atlas sighs. "Tell me if you want to leave. We'll go."

"I can't stay holed up in my room crying all night."

"You can. It's your birthday." He smirks softly. "Cry if you want to—am I right?" He chuckles at his own joke.

"Shh." Nova covers his mouth. "Sometimes it's okay to just be a pretty face, you know? Don't quit your day job, honey."

He glares, biting at her finger.

Her squeals and giggles fill the space. "Hey, it was a joke!" She bats his hands away. "Do not tickle me, ah! I swear to everything good and holy, Atlas Hale I will—*Atlas*!" Nova twists in his arms, her laughter echoing and her grin widening. "Stop! Uncle, oh my gosh."

"Say my jokes are good." Atlas spins her.

"Never!" she shouts.

"Say it."

"Bite me," Nova squeals.

"Careful." He smirks. "Or I might take you up on that offer."

"Is that a promise?" She raises her brow.

Atlas gapes. "You *dirty* dirty little minx."

He's holding her up, breathing harshly as he attempts to catch his breath. Her hands are gripping his biceps and Atlas can't help but feel a sense of déjà vu from their current position. Her cheeks are flushed, and a soft smile is playing on her lips as she reaches her free hand up to brush a strand of hair from his forehead. Atlas tightens his grip on her waist, pulling her closer until she's flush against his chest.

"Do you have any idea," he rasps, "how much I wanted to kiss you that night? Do you know how hard it was for me not to pin you up against the side of that truck and kiss you breathless?"

Her breath hitches at his words, and her chest rises and falls in unison with his own. "You should've." She speaks hardly above a whisper. "I thought you were going to—at least I hoped."

"You would've let me?" He eyes her almost predatorily.

Her eyes train on his Adams's apple. She's too nervous to look him in the face. She can barely even speak; can hardly even get the words out.

"Yes," she whispers.

He looks almost shocked at her words.

"You should've said something." He cups her jaw. "I didn't know," he says truthfully, "I didn't think you wanted me." His lips are ghosting her hairline—peppering over the top of her ear.

Nova shakes her head. "*Idiot*," she mutters. "Of course I want you—wanted you. How could anyone not want you, Atlas?"

"I can think of a lot of people."

She plays with the collar of his shirt, leaning up on her tiptoes to press a kiss to his cheek. "You're everything," she promises.

"I think I could love you one day," he says.

"I know," she whispers, tapping his chest. "Me too."

He kisses her forehead once and again before pulling away. "S'cold," Atlas murmurs. "We should head out back. Everyone's waitin'"

Nova lets her shoulders fall dejected. "Fine," she huffs.

"C'mere." He pulls her close. "You can change your mind."

"No, I need to do this. I've spent the past couple of birthdays stuck in the house. It's time for a change." She slips her hands into his back pockets, her forehead resting against his chest. "I need to move on."

"Grief isn't one size fits all, baby. You're allowed to take as much as you need to digest things. There is no moving on. Not really."

She nods. She knows but, she's felt stuck for two years.

"Let's go." She straightens. "We're already late."

Atlas lets her tug him toward the house. She looks cute with her boots and her oversized sweater. She spent the entire night weaving ribbons through the sleeves. He doesn't get the point, but Nova is worth staying up for—even if it's for nonsense like ribbons in her sleeves.

"I should've worn thicker socks," Nova complains as they move closer. "It's freezing—God, I hate winter so much."

"I told you to wear thicker socks," Atlas points out as he shakes his jacket off. "It's nearly thirty-five degrees right now."

"Are you the weatherman now or something?"

She's arguing with him over her shoulder, so she's hardly even paying attention as she opens the back gate. She completely misses the small crowd of people surrounding a large table filled to the brim with all of her favorite foods and beverages. She misses the twinkle lights strung across the Hawthorne's backyard and the pile of birthday presents.

"Are you going to predict the next snow—"

"*Surprise!*"

She jumps at the rambunctious shouts, and the clambering of

hugs she receives immediately. She's frozen as warmth surrounds her alongside murmurs of best wishes and some sly jokes. It isn't until Atlas presses a kiss to her temple that she realizes she's crying.

"Happy birthday, baby," he whispers.

"How did you—when did you guys even?"

"Atlas set up the whole thing," Indie chimes in. "Mrs. Hawthorne provided the space, but the rest was all Atlas."

"You did this?" She's looking up at him with so much adoration that it makes his chest hurt. "You did all of this for me?"

"I know how hard today was for you. I figured it would be nice to spend it with your friends—the people that love you."

Nova gapes, shaking her head. "Atlas."

"C'mon." Atlas tugs her through the crowd toward the long banquet table near the center of the yard. "Happy birthday."

The cake is small, it's dotted with hearts and flowers and, though a bit smudged—imperfect, she loves it all the same. "It doesn't feel like my birthday," she admits quietly. "It feels like another day to me. You didn't have to do all this, seriously. A cupcake would've been fine."

"The day you were born is definitely a day to celebrate."

She merely shakes her head.

"What are you going to wish for?" he asks, clasping her hands.

The candles twinkle across her face, and as she glances up, Nova can see the smiling faces of her friends. The people who have become something so close to family that it hurts. She sees her mother among these people—in their slight smiles and mixtures of light eyes. She sees Marjorie so evidently. But most of all she sees a love unlike anything she could have ever managed to imagine.

"What else could I ask for?" She tucks herself into his side. "I've got everything that I've ever wanted right here, right now."

And for the first time since her mother passed, Nova feels a reprieve. For once, she feels like everything might be okay. Here beneath sycamore trees, and mayflies—burgundy and flashes of umber, Nova feels the most peace anyone should ever be allowed. For once, Nova is home.

The pair somehow manage to sneak away from the party, and off into his childhood bedroom. He stands nearly embarrassed by the obscene amount of Power Rangers posters littered across the walls, and action figures lying against his old pillows. She quietly laughs.

"Cute, very retro," Nova snorts.

"Shut up," he says, but his smile is evident. "I wanna show you something." Atlas holds out his hand. "You afraid of heights?"

"Um, yes?" Nov says with uncertainty.

"You trust me, right?"

"Always."

The last place Nova expected to be was on top of a roof.

"This is insane. You're insane, Atlas Hale."

He rolls his eyes. "Just don't fall, and you'll be fine."

She blanches. "Oh wow, great pep talk, *Captain Obvious*."

"I won't let you fall," Atlas assures her.

"You better not." She clings to his jacket. "I'll come back and haunt the shit out of you. I can't believe you talked me into this." She heaves. "I'm going to throw up, oh my gosh. Atlas!" Nova yelps when he settles on his back. "You're insane. I'm breaking up with you."

"Shut up, Hawkins, and lay with me." He holds his hand up.

She glances at his hand as if it cursed her out before smacking it away. "Hell no. You're a demon. I'm going to hyperventilate."

"This is the most you've cursed since I've known you."

"Oh, I'm sorry." She sneers. "Am I *bothering* you?"

"Sit down, Nova."

"I—"

He raises his brow.

"I'm sitting down because I'm cold. Not because you told me to."

"Good girl." He smooths her hair down.

"*Bite me.*" She glares.

"Keep talkin' like that and I might finally do it."

She fights back the blush threatening to rise in her cheeks.

As much as she hates the height, Nova can't deny the beauty of the scenery in front of them. Most of the landscaping is dead from the bitter cold, but some of the autumn leaves are still attempting to cling to life among the ashen brown. It's beautiful from up here. Gorgeous.

"It's beautiful," she says quietly.

Their shoulders brush from their proximity, and their fingers interlace. She leans over to rest her head on his shoulder, and for a moment her eyes flutter close. The party was enough to distract her momentarily but—now that the quiet is back, as are her thoughts.

"Atlas."

"Yeah?"

"Can you do something for me?"

"Anything."

The letter burning in her back pocket.

"My mom left me a letter for every birthday that she was going to miss." Nova toys with the paper. It weighs a ton. "I can't read it." She gnaws on her bottom lip, "I was wondering if you…"

He nods before she can even finish. "Of course."

She places it in his hand and swallows thickly.

"Are you sure you don't want Indie or Sienna to do this?"

"No, I need you to do it. *Please.*"

"Are you sure?"

"No." Her hands are shaking. "But I need to do this."

"Nova, I don't know if I should be the one doing this."

"I trust you. Just—*please?*"

The silence lingering among them was thickening, haunting.

"All right." The sound of paper crumbling causes her stomach to instantly knot. "My dearest, Nova…" he begins.

Happy Birthday, angel. There are no words to express the love that I feel for you. You are the best thing that has happened to me in this lifetime. From the moment I saw those two lines on that pregnancy test, I knew that I would love you every day, forever. My dear sweet baby girl, when I was first diagnosed, I was terrified of the life that you would live without me. I was—am far more worried about you than I've ever been for myself. I fear the pain, and the loss that you will experience and how deeply you will feel it. I wish that I was there to tell you how much I love you. You have seen yet another year of expansive growth and exuded beauty. You are the light of my life—my star. My little Nova. I remember trying to name you. I remember how easily it came to me. You are the center of my universe. So I named you Nova. My precious girl, you have a heart forged by the gods; you have a soul that is filled with so much wonder and admiration. All I have ever wanted was to be a mother, and I cannot thank you enough for choosing me to be yours. You are light in this world; I know you are hurting. I know that you feel anger and heartache. But I beg of you, please never lose sight of this world, no matter how callous and riddled with pain it may be. Feel, my little Nova.

Feel deeply and without restraints. Fall in love. ~~*I am sorry.*~~ *I wish you a love that transcends the stars. A love that fills your very soul. If it is possible, as I wish it is—when I am gone from this place, I will be a star. Wish on me. When you are saddened, and you are lost—look to the skies and you will see me there. Among Cassiopeia and Andromeda. I will be there. Live this life of yours, so gracefully and so openly. Love with your entire heart, and when you find love in the ways that I know you will hold fast to it. Hold on to it. Grasps it tightly, my Nova. Love despite the consequences that may come, love with everything you have. The love you have is worth a multitude. Love is the greatest being ever to live so cling to it.* ~~*I'm so so sorry, please forgive me.*~~
I wish you so many beautiful years. So many wonderful moments, my dear. You are a Nova, my love. You are a vesper. Shine bright.
Love always, to the stars and moon,
Your mama

"Nova." He whispers her name so broken, so pained.

Her tears are falling so freely, so openly. Her pain is nearly palpable—it guts him. It tears his heart into pieces. She lets out a choked sob so pained that he has to tear his eyes away. She looks so small.

"Nova." He cups her cheeks. "Baby, *please*."

"How could I wait so long?" She won't open her eyes as she shakes her head. "How could I just ignore her like that?"

"You were hurting—you're allowed to hurt."

"The whole time, she was right there. And I missed it."

"Don't do this to yourself," Atlas pleads.

"I spent so much time being angry with her for leaving when she never even wanted to in the first place. She knew, and she tried to leave me pieces of her. Ignored it for two years. What kind of daughter am I?"

Atlas shakes his head. "Look at me." He tips her chin up. "She loves you. I don't know her, but her words—she loves you. She's here." He places his hand on her chest. "She's always there. I swear it," Atlas whispers, running his thumb along her cheek. "I will love you one day."

She whimpers. "Stop," Nova whispers. "You'll leave. Everyone leaves; my dad, my mom—I have no one left, Atlas. No one."

"No." Atlas clasps her hands. "I *will* love you, Nova Hawkins. One day I'll say it. And I'll mean it. Because you deserve to hear it. You deserve love more than anyone else in this God-forsaken world."

"Atlas…"

He rests her forehead against her own. "I will love you."

"I will love you." She meets his eyes.

"I won't leave. I won't."

"You can't promise that—"

"I won't leave you. Not until something pulls me away."

He thinks he'll love her even then—even in the thereafter.

"Thank you." *For being here*, she wants to say. *For loving me.*

"We're all a little broken," he replies.

"You and me." She smiles softly behind her tears.

"*Always.*"

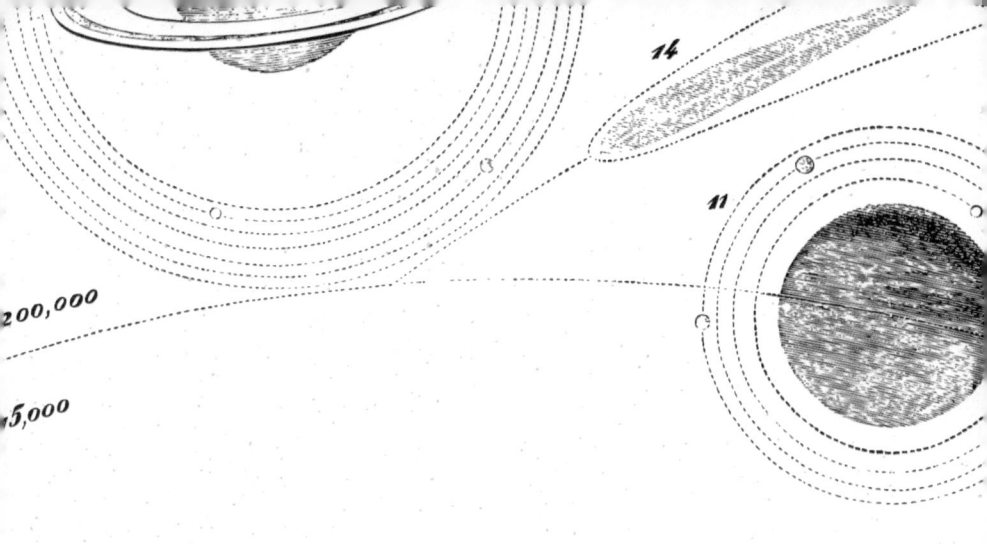

INTERLUDE
i'll keep you safe.

"I think I was made for you," Atlas says randomly three Saturdays before Christmas. "I think someone, somewhere made you for me—and I for you. I think someone must care deeply for me because I'm not sure what I did to deserve you, Nova Hawkins. But I want to keep you here." Atlas gathers her hands in his own. "Right here," he says, placing them against his chest. "Forever if you'll let me."
"Forever sounds pretty good to me," is her only reply.

remnants from chapter seventeen.

"I've never met someone like you before," Atlas says, "and that terrifies me. It absolutely terrifies the living hell out of me, Nova."

She turns her head to look at him. "Every time I'm around you it feels like my heart might beat out of my chest. And that terrifies me."

Their pinkies touch slightly.

"Then I guess we can just be terrified together," Atlas concludes.

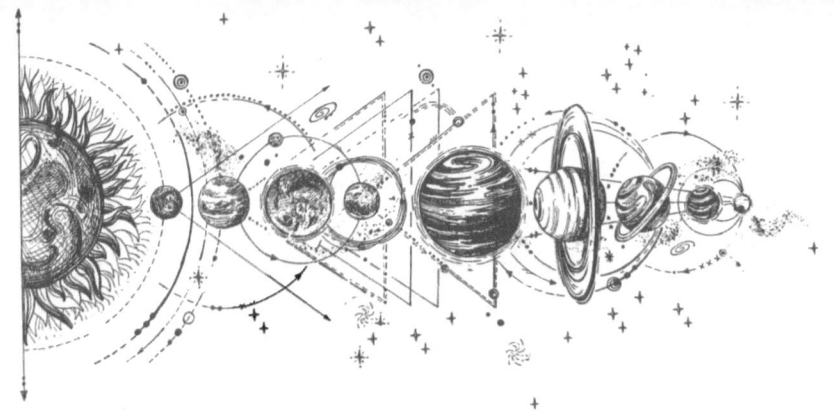

chapter twenty-four
darlin' i'd wait for you

Atlas remembers. He remembers the night that he had first laid eyes on Nova Hawkins; how her hair fell in flurries at her shoulders. He remembers her slight smile, the flush of red that filled her cheeks from the evening cold. Atlas can remember the way that she spoke of the stars. He can remember becoming instantly enamored by her presence, perhaps even a bit uncomfortable all at the same time, but he remembers leaving the park that night and not feeling so alone if only for a second. The loneliness returned the next day, of course, but that night he felt okay.

Atlas Hale is a haunted soul; haunted by the demons of his past. He is surrounded by the remnants of his upbringing and defined by his parents. And every single day, he wonders if and when he'll end up like them. He remembers in high school when they had a lesson in science class about adaptation—and how centuries ago animals shifted their appearances, their diets, and ways of living to adapt to

their environments. From that day forward Atlas was convinced that he would end up a product of his environment. So he stopped caring as much about proving his parents wrong. He got into fights at school and was arrested far too many times than he wanted to count. He attempted to ignore the Hawthornes and all of their kindness toward him because he would end up just like his father. He was a product of his parents.

He would become them.

It was a fear that he carried with him for the entirety of his life. It didn't stop until the one day when Catie pulled him aside and ripped him a new one. She told him that life was far more than the pain that followed it, and that there were people that cared about him and loved him; that he didn't need to conform to what everyone expected him to do. That he could be Atlas—just Atlas, not Darren's kid or Abigail's mistake.

Just Atlas.

There were only a few people that saw him as just Atlas. And Nova was one of them. She saw outside his pain. She only saw him. From the moment that they had met all those many nights ago, Nova had always only seen him. And that was terrifying. He figures that's why he pushed away in the beginning, why he detested their friendship so much.

She made him feel like he wasn't a mistake; like he was more than just his parents. She had seen him that night among his pain, and she smiled. She smiled, and she spoke of the stars as though they were friends, like they were wayward entities. For that reason, Atlas eventually stopped trying to stay away from Nova. It hadn't been like, or even love, no that came *much*, much later but he figures it acute admiration.

He remembers when he first met her. He can remember the smell of her perfume and the soft smile that graced her face. How she tilted her head back to look up at the stars with such a love that it left him breathless. He remembers climbing into his truck afterward and driving home to his apartment. He remembers the lamp that he forgot to turn off, the way he stubbed his toe because evening waned so heavily in the space. He remembers it all. He likes to think back to the night they met with such gratitude and thankfulness because he doesn't know how or exactly why it happened. But he thinks someone, somewhere must care a great deal about him to allow him to be in her life. He must have done something right—perhaps the universe didn't hate him after all.

Atlas shakes his head and glances up from his drawing. There are flurries in the air and Nova is standing outside—her hands outstretched, a look of endless wonder on her face. And he can't help but think about how much has changed. How much he loves her. How suddenly it had happened. She runs up to the truck window, tapping softly. "Come on."

Atlas can hardly deny her anything, even if he wanted to. So he discards his notepad and opens the driver-side door stepping out into the cold air. "It's freezing," he points out as she tugs him closer.

She hardly hears him as she glances up at the sky, "It's beautiful," Nova marvels. "What did we ever do to deserve this?"

His eyes are only on her though. "I don't know," he admits. "I've never felt more unworthy of something in my entire life."

His change in tone causes her to glance at him. There's a soft smile on his face when she looks at him, and his eyes are slightly red. "You deserve far more in this world than you think, Atlas Hale."

He shakes his head. "I don't deserve you."

"You do," she counters despite his objections.

"You're a once-in-a-lifetime sort of thing, Nova."

Her combat boots dig into the dampening ground as she rises to her toes. She taps once, and then twice on his chest. It's their way of saying it without ever having to. His fingers comb through her hair, gathering at the nape of her neck before he too repeats the same motion.

He loves her, in every sense of the word. But saying it, he just can't. Everyone he has ever openly loved has left him. And he can't lose her. So instead he nods once, and again before lowering his forehead to her own and clenching his eyes shut. *"Nova..."* he whispers.

"I know," she murmurs, "I promise I know."

"For as long as you'll let me," he says.

"That's a really long time, Hale. You're stuck with me."

Atlas presses a kiss to her nose, before saying, "I'm sorry that I can't say it." He looks anguished, upset with himself. "You deserve it."

"I'll wait. I'll wait for you, as long as it takes."

"I'm sorry," he repeats.

"I'll wait," Nova tells him, "I'll wait for you."

And he knows she means it.

Atlas remembers the night they met with such fondness. He remembers everything. He always will. Nova is a once-in-a-lifetime person; she is his, and he is hers. He remembers, he always will.

chapter twenty-five
rhea

It's fragile, Nova notes, time. She blinks and the seconds have passed with such an obscurity that she can hardly even keep up. She feels like she's lost something every other minute of the day. Like time is no longer within reach and before she knows it everything will have ceased to exist and somehow slip away. Nova has always been a wanderer, a candescent soul. She's always felt somewhat lost in the world around her, always five feet behind everyone else. She was constantly tumbling to keep up, and truth be told, she wasn't sure that she ever would.

"I have to go," she tells Atlas's nearly sleeping form.

The sun has disappeared altogether, replaced with an ink-dark shadow and the clock beside his bed now reads one in the morning.

"Stay," he murmurs sleepily against her neck, "Please."

So she lays there for a bit, toying with the ends of his hair while his eyes flutter closed again. She's lost in the atlas of his body: his taunt jaw, his furrowed brow, and his dimpled chin. He has a birthmark on his arm that he once concluded looked like a rhea though Nova can't really see it. She's lost in him, but somehow found all in the same. Nova loves him, she loves him always, even if they're both a bit broken.

Eventually, she's lulled away by the soft sound of his breathing.

"Good morning." He traces the side of her face. "So beautiful."

"Mmm." She smiles with her eyes closed. "Morning."

"You stayed." Their legs are intertwined beneath the sheets, and her thighs are cold to the touch. "Didn't think you would."

"Where else would I go?"

He runs his thumb along her brow and shrugs.

"You look cute when you sleep," she tells him. "Peaceful."

His eyes are haunted, they always have been. But the darkness seems to fade from his face when he's sleeping; she wishes he'd look like that all the time. Wishes that his demons would see the light for once.

"I don't sleep that well most nights."

"Promise me you'll call me when you can't."

He nods, but they both know it's a lie. He won't burden her.

Atlas sends her a weak smile tapping one, and then again on the place above her heart. She presses a kiss to his lips and says, *"Always."*

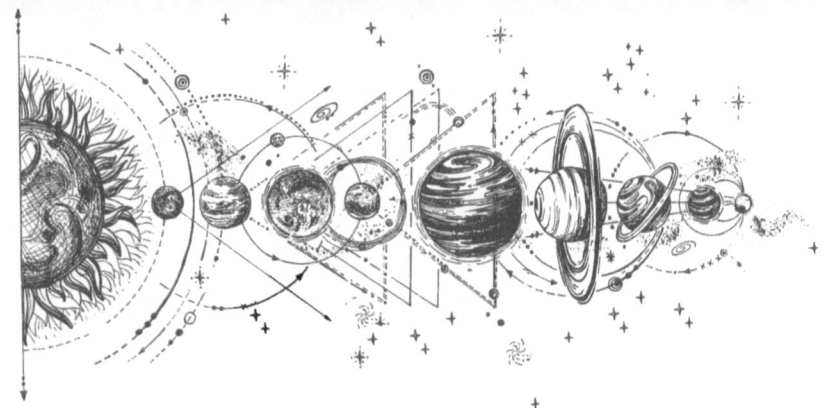

chapter twenty-six
a soft epilogue.

Nova has always been fascinated by the concept of an epilogue. It seems to her like the perfect way to round off a story. And she remembers the time when her mother, Marjorie, explained to her what an epilogue was. Marjori told her that it was the ending of one story, and the beginning of another. Nova has always been captivated by this idea. Her mother told her that she deserved nothing less than a *peaceful* epilogue. That she deserves a story that ended with hope, and a love that transcends the ages. For the vast majority of her life, Nova never believed she would ever obtain anything close to that. Never believed that she would ever be worthy of a love so pure, and grounded.

But that all changed when she met Atlas.

I love you, she said one week after Christmas. "I *love* you."

"Nova…" He held her so close, so tightly, as though he wished to

forge himself into her. Like he never wanted to let go. His hands shook as they grasped hers in his own. He placed her hands against his chest and held them there. His eyes shined with such sincerity, with so much love and gratitude. He loved her. She knew it—he always has.

"Here." He placed an origami heart in her hand.

"What is this?" she asked.

"My heart," he said. "I've never been the best with words. I've never felt love in my life. No one has ever loved me enough. No one has ever wanted to, not until you. And I know how I feel and I need you to know it even if I can't say it right now. I do feel it." He nodded. "I will keep you here"—he tapped his chest—"for the rest of my life if you allow me to. I will..." Atlas struggled for the words but she knew. She knew. Atlas was her ending, and he was her beginning.

"Thank you." She sent him a teary smile. "Thank you."

Atlas was her beginning and her ending.

He was her *epilogue*.

PART FOUR,
the paradigm of love.

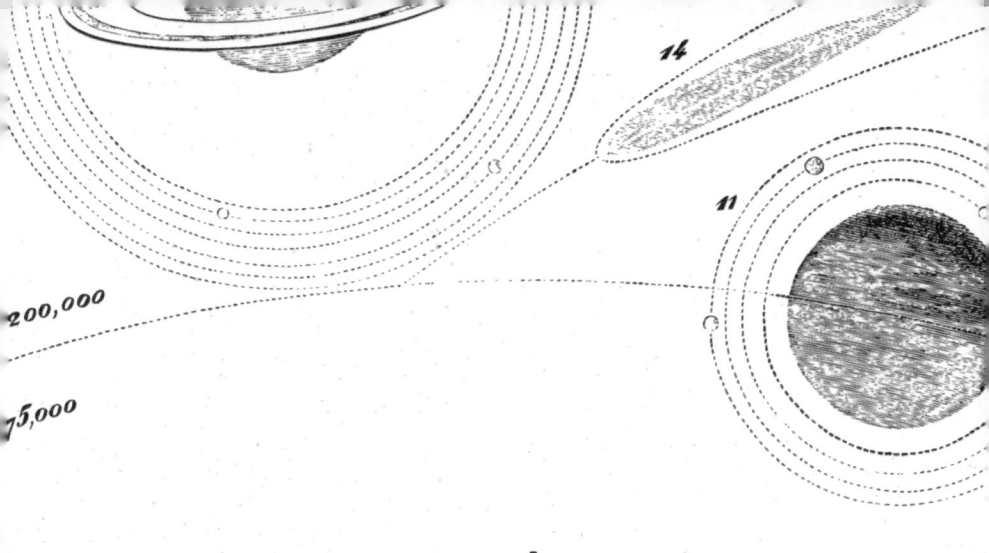

When

He says it on their two-month anniversary. His palms are shaking profusely, nearly embarrassingly, as he all but sputters the words out.

"I love you," he says one evening. "I love you, Nova Hawkins."

She doesn't say much because she knows. Nova has known all along. "I know," she says. "Thank you for trusting me with your heart. Thank you for trusting me to love you back."

It's easy with Nova—it always has been. So easy, like breathing. Loving Nova is second nature to Atlas. It's the only thing that's ever come easily to him in his entire life. Loving her was a privilege, an honor. Being loved by Nova was far more than anyone should ever be bestowed. Her love was the kind that transcended time and space. It was soft and gentle. When Nova loved—she did it with her entire being; she did it fully without attempting to ever hold it back or censor it.

"I love you," he whispers. "More than you'll ever know."

"Love you," she murmurs against his lips.

And that's enough for him. It's simple, a bit chaotic but it's them.

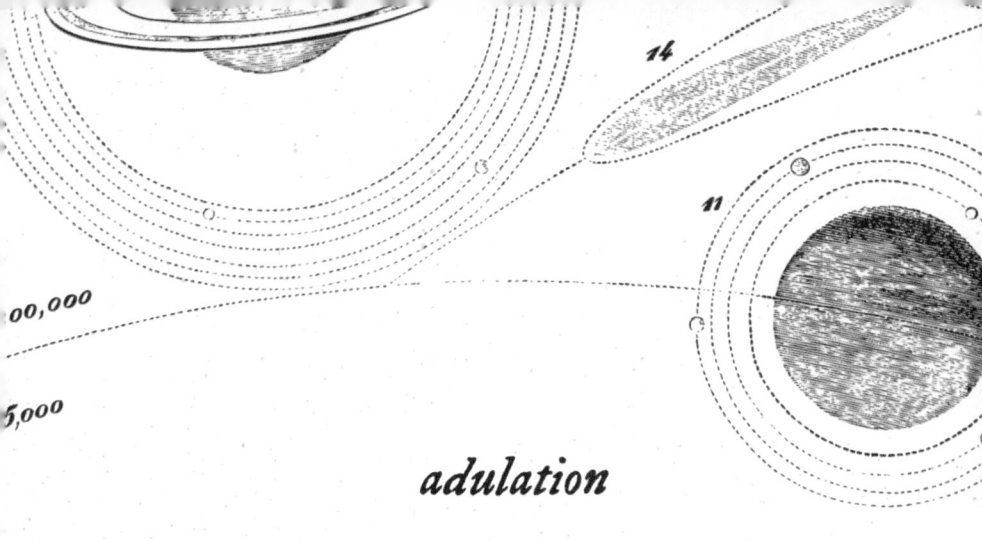

adulation

There was no *before* him.

There would be no after him either. There simply *was*. Nova would come to explain it as a cosmic event that transcended the ages. She would remember the rickety swing set that creaked in the background of their beginning. She would remember the chirping of the wayward birds that sang praises to their communion and fortitude. Nova Hawkins would never forget the moment his cerulean—swimming to the brim with tethered pain and unspoken agony—gaze met her own. There was no before him. There would be no after him. There was oblivion—a moment between before and after—a moment between what she believed to be serenity and damnation. That is where Atlas and Nova dwell. That is where they would stay because a life without Atlas Hale is meaningless. To Nova, all life deserves meaning. So, she never pondered before him. Atlas Hale came into her life in the semblance of a destructive tornado; he had unearthed her, *ruined* her. There was no before him. She simply could not fathom the thought of it. There was no before, there simply was. There was Atlas, and there was Nova, and that was enough.

the end

acknowledgements

When I first started writing this book I was grappling with grief. I was in a place in my life where I wasn't entirely sure I would ever recover from. This book, and these characters have been my closest friends and an extension of my innermost pain and suffering. This is a story that I am so passionate about and have loved so deeply. I am so excited to finally be able to share it with you all, whoever might be reading this story.

Thank you first to God, for being everything to me. I am nothing without you, and I never will be. Thank you for saving me.

To my parents for aiding my book addiction, and loving me. Thank you for encouraging me in everything that I've ever done. For being there through every moment in my life when I should've never gotten back up again. This book, and everything that I do is for you. You are far more than I could have ever prayed for and I am blessed to have you as my parents. I love you unconditionally with all of my being.

Thank you to the people who have championed me forward. To the friend's I have made along the way in this journey who have continuously uplifted me and been a shoulder to cry on in my most frustrating moments of doubt while writing this novel.

Thank you to my amazing beta readers for giving me so much confidence in this story and being my biggest supporters. You're the kindest souls I have ever had the pleasure of meeting. Thank you as well to my street team who have brought so many new people to this story.

Thank you to Emma, my editor for taking the time to clean up all of my grammatical issues and mistakes until this book was something worth putting out there and publishing. You are the most patient person ever.

And lastly, to me. It has been such a long time coming. You have gone through the hardest moments, the most overwhelming hardships ever and you continue to push forward. I am so proud of you. I am so excited to see where this world takes you. You did it. You poured your heart and soul into something and saw it through to the end. When everyone around you said that you couldn't, you did it.

about the author

Liliana Hastings is a twenty-two year old indie author who finds herself continuously immersed in books. After spending her early adolescence writing, she finally decided to give the world insight into her oasis. When Ana is not writing, she often spends her time frequenting coffee shops and visiting local bookstores in her hometown. She seeks solace amongst the simpler things in life, cherishing the moments when she can spend time with family and those closest to her. The author is an avid lover of all things whimsical and cozy. You will most likely find her watching the Harry Potter movies with a hot cup of coffee despite the season or temperatures.

Liliana loves to hear from her readers and can be reached on any of her social media accounts.

www.ingramcontent.com/pod-product-compliance
Lightning Source LLC
LaVergne TN
LVHW041759060526
838201LV00046B/1048